HANDLE
WITH FEAR

HANDLE WITH FEAR

THOMAS B. DEWEY

#4 in the Singer Batts series

WILDSIDE PRESS

CHAPTER I

The first one, the younger one, checked in about five-thirty in the afternoon. The second, a man-of-the-world type, maybe thirty-eight, came in later, around seven. Harry Baird, the day clerk, checked the first one in and Jack Pritchard, night man, came on duty just before the second guy stepped up to the desk.

That would be the reason I was there both times. I always check up just before dinner and again at the time when Pritchard comes to work. I like to get a picture in my mind of how many people we have, where they are and who paid in advance and who didn't.

I got pretty sharp pictures of these two boys. For one thing they carried suitcases that looked identical. Inexpensive, standard and pretty well put together. They were both saddle tan with bright brass fasteners. There was nothing much unusual in the suitcases alone. Big manufacturers sell a lot of luggage. But there were the other facts: (1) they were strangers, (2) they came in close together, (3) they both registered from Chicago and (4) they both paid in advance.

The first lad, the younger one, came in like a cross-country runner at the end of the race; stubborn, but dragging. The suitcase wasn't heavy—I helped him with it—but you could see by the way he carried it that he'd had enough. His shirt collar was open and he walked heavily on his heels. But it was his face that really gave him away. It was beat, completely. When he reached out to sign the registration card, he swayed and his hand shook. He didn't look around or say anything except that he wanted a room with a shower. He just signed the card, paid his money, picked up the suitcase and waited for somebody to show him where to go. Underneath the three days' beard and the hollow, hunted eyes, he was a clean-looking kid. Harry Baird took him up to his room on the third floor.

This other one, the second guy, walked in as if he knew where he was going all right and you couldn't tell by his face whether he liked it or not. He walked tightly, all in one piece, and he carried the suitcase as if it was nothing at all. He was stocky, well-built, with hard gray eyes and a weather-beaten face. His clothes were good and his hand didn't shake when he signed the register. His money was just as genuine as the kid's money and he looked as if he had more of it.

But his face bothered me. It was wrong. I don't know exactly how you tell, but you do tell. It was a wrong face and I didn't like it. Maybe it was the faint scar, a thin white line twisting down from the corner of his mouth across his chin. However, in the hotel business you don't turn anybody away just because he's got a scar.

Nevertheless, I kept remembering them and their identical suitcases and the fact that they were both from Chicago, and that they had both paid in advance. Nobody asked them to pay in advance.

Their names on the register were: Number One—Jay Perry; Number Two—Arch Whitney.

I remembered them with the rear part of my mind while I ate a late dinner in the dining room and checked over the day's business. We had almost eighty percent occupancy that night, which was good, and I wished we could keep it up. Business had not been so good. In the past week it had picked up and I hoped the average would stay high. But you couldn't tell. In a little town like Preston, which is not even on a main highway, you have to depend on steady customers, like salesmen and seasonal workers. The only casual trade comes from people who get sleepy and turn off the main highway three miles south of town when they see our sign with the big red arrow.

The dinner was good and afterward I went out to the lobby and chinned with a couple of local merchants, and then I went into the suite and on into my bedroom and packed a few things for our trip to Chicago the next day.

It was a quiet night and because business was good and I was going on a trip the next day and one thing and another, I felt fine. I started to sing. I sang about four bars of "Wait Till the Sun Shines, Nellie," and then a quiet, firm voice in the living room of the suite said, "Joseph."

I went to the bedroom door and looked out.

"Yeah, Singer," I said.

"Please spare me that base baritone."

"Excuse me," I said. "I feel good."

"I am glad."

"When I feel good, I like to sing."

"At almost any other time I would be happy to indulge you. Tonight, however, I am somewhat heavily engaged."

"Congratulations," I said. "Have you got to the part yet where the dog rescues his master from a watery grave by dragging him onto an ice floe?"

"Unfortunately, the Bard of Avon introduced no such telling incidents into his frequently melodramatic climaxes."

He was talking pretty stiff and I decided to leave him alone. He was putting final touches on a paper he would read the next day to a bunch of Shakespeare scholars at the University of Chicago.

That would be the reason for our trip. We would drive up in the morning. Singer would go to the Shakespeare meetings in the afternoon and evening and I would go here and there according to what developed. We would stay with one of the professors that night and return the next day. A short trip, but a welcome change, such as we get once in a great while when Singer Batts goes out in the world.

I glanced over his shoulder at the papers on the old desk by the window. They were covered with notes and scratched-out portions and numbers, and I couldn't see how he would be able to make any sense out of it when he began to read it.

"Why don't you get some girl to type that up for you?" I asked.

He didn't look up but I saw the horror slide across his face.

"Out of the question," he said. "She'd never follow my copy."

"Can you follow it?"

"Quite easily, thank you. Because I know what's in it."

"All right."

So I left him alone. I looked back once as I went into the bedroom. He was hunched down over the desk, his thin hair rumpled, his frayed old bathrobe sitting up around him, his long chin sticking out, pointing at the papers. He would sit there all night, then grab a cat nap and be fresh as the morning dew when it was time to leave. Sleep and food he ignores. Singer Batts, more than anyone else I ever knew, lives on what's in his mind. I never really believed it was possible till I met him. One lucky day.

But me, I like to get my sleep. So I shut up my suitcase, parked it on the floor, took a shower and went to bed. I refrained from singing in the shower.

* * * *

It was about two o'clock in the morning when I woke up. I lay there for a couple of minutes, trying to figure out why and then, out of habit, I put on my pants and shoes and went out to the lobby.

Jack Pritchard was reading a magazine. The lights were low and it was quiet.

"Tell me why I suddenly woke up," I said to him.

Jack, who figures me for an intruder in Singer Batts' hotel, where Jack has worked for twenty-five years—ten for Singer and fifteen for Singer's old man, Emory Batts—didn't even look up.

"I couldn't say," he said.

"There must have been a reason."

"Possibly you ate too much lemon pie," he said.

He always riles me.

"Get your nose out of the magazine and tell me what's wrong," I said.

He looked up slowly.

"Mr. Spinder—" he began in that haughty tone and I cut him off quick.

"All right," I said.

I went out to the kitchen. I poured a glass of milk and drank it slowly, standing in the dark, listening.

I finished the milk, put the glass down and went out into the corridor. I went to the back stairs and stood there, listening. After a couple of minutes, I started up the steps slowly, stepping on the extreme sides where they didn't creak. I got to where I could look along the second-floor corridor and I took a long look and then a step creaked above me.

I ducked back down to the ground floor and slid into the service closet in the rear vestibule. Our back door opens onto an alley and beyond the alley is the small hotel parking lot.

The service closet has a sliding door and I left it open far enough for me to look out but not far enough for anyone to look in, unless he pressed his eyeball against the crack. The vestibule was lighted by a red exit light.

A couple of more steps creaked and it was a long time before anybody showed. I was in no mood to have to accost anybody for jumping his bill, and on the other hand I was in no mood to let him get away with it either.

But this guy's bill had already been paid.

It was the kid who had checked in at five-thirty, the one called Jay Perry. He came down the stairs, fully dressed, lugging the bag, creeping down as quietly as he could manage, one hand against the wall to steady himself. The exit light glowed red on his face.

I had no reason not to let him go. He'd paid. If he wanted to leave in the middle of the night by the back door, it was up to him. It wasn't the conventional way to leave a hotel, but I'm no stickler for convention, if the bill is paid.

He cleared the last step and started across the vestibule to the back door. He hadn't quite made it when the steps began to creak again. The kid heard it. He stopped, looked once over his shoulder, hitched up the suitcase and made for the door. I let him go and watched the steps again. The door banged open as the kid went out and then this second guy, Arch Whitney, came down the last few steps fast.

He had something shiny in his right hand and his suitcase in the other. The shiny thing was a gun. I saw his face flash past me. The door had swung to before he reached it and, with both hands full, he had some trouble getting it open. I stepped out of the closet.

"Let me help," I said.

He swung around and took a poke at me. I ducked in time and the gun in his hand grazed the side of my head.

"Stop it," I said. "I was just going to open the door for you. Hell of a way to leave the hotel."

He went to the door again and I reached in front of him and pushed it open. He ran out into the alley, stopped and looked both ways.

"He went thataway," I said, pointing both ways.

Then, looking beyond him into the parking lot, I saw the Perry kid moving behind the cars, still creeping. He was working his way toward the west side of the hotel. When he got to the end of the line of parked cars he would have to come back into the alley at the far end. There was no other place to go.

This Whitney was standing in the alley, looking around.

"Listen," he said quietly. "I'm a cop. That man is wanted in Chicago."

"All right," I said. "Go get him."

"Look," he said. "Give me some help. I'll go this way." He pointed toward the east end of the alley, toward the street. "And you go that way. We'll find him. He's not driving a car."

"Sure," I said and stepped into the alley.

He walked along toward the street, looking around as he went. I started up the alley in the other direction. There was no hurry. That was the way the kid was going and when he got back into the alley at the west end, he would either have to stop or go straight up. The alley ends in a pocket with buildings on all sides. You can't get out of there unless you can scale a brick wall, in which the lowest window is ten feet off the ground. I know you can't do it carrying a suitcase.

I caught up with him at the moment he realized what he was up against. He had surveyed all the walls and he had turned back toward the alley. The suitcase was dragging at his right shoulder when I walked up to him.

He looked at me, startled for a moment, then he kind of pulled himself together in the shoulders, ducked his head and lit out to his left toward the parking lot, still lugging the suitcase.

This made no sense. Either he was out on his feet and didn't know what he was doing, or he was trying to run into something that would finish it all up for good.

I started across the parking lot after him, trotting, and just as he reached the street—Oak Street, it is, running north out of town—Whitney came around the corner out of the alley and got in his way.

I was ten or fifteen feet away when Whitney lifted his arm and slugged the kid in the side of the head. The Perry boy fell down on the pavement. I caught up with him and Whitney was bending down, reaching for a handful of shirt. I stepped over the kid and joggled Whitney with my elbow.

"Hold it," I said. "What's the problem here?"

The guy was impatient.

"I told you," he said. "This man is wanted in Chicago. I have to bring him in."

"You're on the police force in Chicago?"

"Yes," he said.

"Then you'll have a badge or something."

"Sure I have."

"Let's see it."

"It's in the suitcase. It'll take time—"

"In the suitcase!"

"Sure—"

"Hell of a place for a badge. Move over."

I took over his suitcase, released the catch and opened it. It was empty. It was brand-new and completely empty, except for the tissue paper they sometimes put inside—God knows why.

Up to now it had just been a hunch. But when I asked him for a badge there wasn't any reason why he shouldn't produce it. It seemed silly to carry it around in a suitcase.

I gave him a push. I pushed kind of hard. He sat down on the pavement, cursing. Perry was trying to get up under my feet and I stepped aside and gave him room.

The guy on the ground looked up and swore some more. The kid grabbed his suitcase again and lit out for the back corner of the hotel, toward Front Street, Preston's main drag.

"You let him get away," the other one said.

"Maybe he deserves to get away."

"Ahh!" he said.

He scrambled to his feet and picked up his empty suitcase. He ran off around the corner, following the kid, and I went back into the hotel through the rear door. It was a shorter route to Front Street, where I knew they would both wind up.

I looked out the front door of the hotel and the kid was across the street now and the so-called cop was standing near the hotel steps and they were staring at each other. The cop lifted his hand and I saw that gun again.

I pushed open the door and hollered. There was a shot and I saw the kid drop to his knees. I ran down the steps and up behind the marksman and hit him with my shoulder in the small of the back. He let out a grunt and fell on his face. I went across the street, but the kid had got up by now and was running again, west, out of town this time, toward the bridge over the creek and the county road. I pounded after him, not knowing why.

At the end of the row of business buildings, just before the bridge, where a vacant lot straggles down into Front Street, he dropped the suitcase and flopped to his knees again. When I caught up with him he was holding his head in both hands, trembling, making low sounds in his throat.

I touched his shoulder. He looked up, started to his feet, saw he couldn't make it and went back to his knees. I gave him a hand and he stood up all right. His breath came in jerks. I looked around and the other guy was not in sight.

"All right," the kid said. "You've got me. Let's get it over with."

"Did he hit you?" I asked.

He shook his head.

"I'm just pooped," he said.

"Is he a cop?"

"I don't know. He might be."

"What do we do now?"

"It's up to you," he said. "Just let's not fool around over it."

He was certainly very young, very scared and very tired. "I'd like to hear the story," I said.

He shrugged.

"Come on," I said. "We'll walk slow. Maybe Singer Batts will be through working by the time we get there."

"Who?" he said.

"Singer Batts," I said.

CHAPTER II

We went into the lobby, me carrying the suitcase. Whitney was standing there by the desk. Jack Pritchard sat on the stool behind the desk, looking pained. Whitney reached out toward the kid with a set of handcuffs.

"Thanks for the help," he said. "I'll take over."

"Not yet," I said. "I want to hear the story—from him. Put those things back in your pocket."

"Now listen—"

"Jack," I said to Pritchard, "call George Cooler."

This was something Jack was happy to do. He picked up the phone and asked the operator for George Cooler, our town marshal.

Perry, the kid, was leaning against the desk, still panting. The other one stood there with his handcuffs, looking like a sorehead.

The front door opened and big George Cooler came in, gazing at us out of his knobby red face.

"George," I said, "this gentleman is annoying my guests. Lock him up for the night."

George was doubtful.

"I don't know—"

"Look," Whitney said, "I'm a policeman from Chicago. I have to bring this man in. He's wanted—"

"Tell it to George," I said. "You must have papers somewhere. Get them out."

"If you throw me in the can," he said, "I'll sue for false arrest."

"Sure," I said. "Tomorrow. Take him away, George."

"Well, Joe, he might sue us at that."

"Then get him out of the hotel. Just get him away from here."

"Don't push," the guy said. "I'll go. But you'll regret it."

"Sure," I said.

He leaned down and picked up one of the identical bags and started out.

"Just a minute," I said, going after him. "You've got the wrong luggage."

"I know my own bag," he said.

I took it out of his hand.

"We'll see," I said. "Yours was empty. Witness this, George."

I set the suitcase down and opened it.

It wasn't empty. It wasn't jammed full, either. You didn't have any trouble closing the lid. But it was solidly packed.

Packed with money. Long green. Currency. About a quarter of a million bucks' worth.

Everybody was still. The "cop" stood beside me, looking down. George Cooler stood, bent over, staring at the suitcase. Jack Pritchard sat stiff and straight on his stool staring straight ahead. The youngster leaned against the desk, watching my face.

I watched his.

The cop finally spoke.

"See?" he said. "It was a holdup. Now, if you don't mind—" I waved my hand to shut him up.

"George," I said, "go get Amos Bittner. Tell him we've got a bunch of loose money here and it looks as if his bank would be the safest place for it. You help him count it."

George went out. I was still watching the kid by the desk. He looked right back at me without batting an eye. Finally I straightened up and looked at the "cop" again.

"If it was a holdup," I said, "you could have said so before. If you were a real cop, you wouldn't have to pull any such stuff as carrying your identification around in empty suitcases. You can stay or go—as you please. But stay out of my hair till I get word from Chicago."

"I'll go," he said, "and to hell with it."

"Good night," I said.

He went out, letting the door slam behind him. I walked to the desk.

"Come on in," I said.

The Perry kid looked up, dazed.

"What?"

"We'll go in here and have a stiff drink."

He went along with me into the suite. He sat down in the first chair he came to and I mixed a couple of drinks. He drank in a hurry, coughing a little.

"Thanks," he said.

"Now, what's the story?" I said.

Singer Batts was still hunched over the desk, scratching on his paper. I knew talking wouldn't bother him. The kid was staring at him.

"It's Singer Batts," I said. "Don't worry about him."

The kid looked up at me finally. He had straight black hair, combed straight back. It was a little too long now, curling up at the back of his neck. His eyes were blue and he had freckles on his nose. Now under his eyes there were black circles that didn't belong there. His complexion was pasty and his face drawn-up and stiff. Whatever he'd been doing the last few days—it had left the marks on him.

"I'm on the run," he said.

"How long?" I asked.

"Twenty-four hours. From Chicago."

"What are you running from?"

"Cops, mostly. I had to. There wasn't any other way."

"What do you mean 'cops mostly'?"

"Somebody else, too. Gangsters—something—I don't know for sure."

"What did you do?"

"Nothing. Somebody else did. I've got to find out."

"Well, what happened to anybody?"

"Murder happened. To my wife."

There was a silence.

"Sorry," I said.

"It's all right. It's too late to worry about that. I might as well tell you about it. Only—if I hadn't got caught here I was going back after I got a little sleep. I was going back there and straighten things out."

"Maybe you can make it yet."

"You'll have to turn me in."

"I don't have to do anything. What's the story?"

I gave him another drink and he drank it and thought things over for a while and then he told me the story.

He was in the service and when he got out he went to Washington, D. C., and got a job in Civil Service, something in the Labor Department. Just an ordinary kind of job, a clerk. His real name was Nick Andrews.

After a while he met a girl there, a girl named Constancia Perotta, a war widow. They got married. Constancia worked for the Agriculture Department. After they were married, she worked for a while and then Nick convinced her she ought to quit. She was a good wife, took good care of the apartment and cooked good meals. They got along all right.

But she wasn't the kind of a girl who could sit around all day and all night and be happy with the housework. She wanted more activity.

He tried to keep up with her, took her out evenings, dancing and one thing and another. It cost money and he didn't make such a lot. But when she wanted to go back to work he wouldn't hear of it. She wanted a new dress that cost a hundred dollars and he said he couldn't afford it. The next day she went out and bought the dress and was wearing it when he got home from work. He was tired and he shot off his mouth. She let him make his speech and then she said, "This dress didn't cost you a nickel. I paid for it myself."

When he wanted to know where she got the money, she wouldn't tell him. He stormed around for a while and she let him work off the steam and then cuddled up to him and the thing got smoothed over for that night.

Then something else came up that she wanted and the same thing happened. She still wouldn't tell him about the money and they got into quite a fight. They lived in a small apartment with thin walls and after they'd yelled at each other for a while some neighbor came to the door and asked them to go fight somewhere else.

This was when the telephone rang. Nick went to it and some man on the other end asked for Constancia. Nick hung up on him.

He was worked up plenty by now and this got him more upset than ever. He demanded to know who the guy was who was calling his wife on the phone. Naturally he wanted to know. But Constancia was upset too and she decided not to talk.

Nick did what guys usually do in that situation. He went out and got drunk and wound up in a little hotel somewhere and slept it off till around noon the next day. He called the office and said he was sick and he wandered around town by himself, trying to work up enough nerve to go back home.

He finally made it late in the afternoon and when he got there, Constancia was gone. She was gone with clothes and luggage. Home to mother. Except she didn't have a mother to go to.

She did leave a note. It wasn't an unfriendly note, just lonely and scared-sounding.

"Darling," the note said, "I tried to find you, but I didn't know where you'd gone. I had to leave in a hurry. I'm going to Chicago. I'll come back. I'm going to stay with Marcella. But don't come there. If anything should happen to me, get in touch with Marcella later. I love you."

Nick checked all the trains and busses and planes. He finally found out she had taken a plane early that afternoon to Chicago. He borrowed some money from a friend and took the first plane he could get—also to Chicago.

He remembered that Constancia had told him not to go to her sister Marcella's place. But he had that address and nothing else to go on, so that's where he went. Constancia was there.

Besides Constancia and her sister, there was another guy there, a young, dark Italian named Angelo. He didn't like Nick and Nick didn't like him. They stayed away from each other.

He could see that Constancia was upset and he tried to get her to talk to him, but she wouldn't say anything at all. Neither would Marcella. He didn't get to first base. He tried everything he could think of, and finally he got sore again and there was another squabble and he walked out. He was a great guy for walking out at the wrong time.

Later he got sorry again and went back to Marcella's. She worked nights, in a club of some kind, and she and the Italian were gone. But Constancia was there. She was there and she was dead. She'd been strangled. There were the marks on her throat and she wasn't breathing any more.

He didn't know what to do. So he just sat there. He sat until three-thirty in the morning when Marcella and her boyfriend, Angelo, got home. Marcella told Nick to call the police. But Angelo went over and jerked the telephone wire out of the box and said to hell with that, just stay right there until he got back. He gave Marcella a gun and told her to hold Nick there.

Marcella told Nick that she knew he hadn't killed Constancia, but Angelo thought he probably had. Angelo was more dangerous than the cops. He worked for the biggest mob in the world and the reason he had left was to report to his boss, the big boss, and Marcella said Nick would be better off in jail than in the hands of the mob. But he couldn't call the cops now, or it would get Marcella in trouble too. So the only thing for him to do was to hide out. She gave him quite a pitch. She sold him. Then she made him knock her out with the gun. And he did it and ran.

When he left the apartment, he noticed this car parked out in front and that it began to follow him. He went downtown and got a bus and started back east. The bus stopped a couple of times and both times it stopped, he saw this car with the same guy in it. He knew he was being followed. So he got off the bus at the crossroads three miles south of Preston and walked into town.

But when he came into the hotel, he saw his shadow was still with him. That's why he tried to sneak out in the middle of the night.

* * * *

"Because—" he said, "I had to get back to Chicago."

"Why?" I asked.

"I realized after a while that I was just running away. Marcella might need help. I ought to tell the police. I ought to find out who killed my wife. It was silly to run away."

I thought about it.

"You figured you could solve it all by yourself?" I asked.

"I didn't figure I could, but I figured I ought to try."

"I see," I said.

I mixed another drink. I glanced over at the desk. Singer Batts was still hunched over it, but he had laid down his pencil and he wasn't scratching on the paper any more.

"You heard this?" I asked.

"Yes, Joseph," he said quietly.

He turned slowly and looked at Nick Andrews for the first time. Andrews looked back at him. The kid looked kind of startled.

"This is Singer Batts," I said. "He owns the hotel. My name is Joe Spinder. I'm the manager."

"Thanks for listening, anyway," Nick said.

"The story is true?" Singer asked him.

Nick looked straight into his face.

"It's true, so help me," he said.

"And Chicago is your goal?"

"That's right."

Singer looked at me.

"Then I see no reason why we shouldn't take Mr. Andrews to Chicago with us in the morning."

"Neither do I," I said.

Nick looked at us blankly.

"But how can you do this?" he said. "There may be bulletins out for me. The police must know about Constancia now."

Singer waved his hand briefly.

"Alarums and excursions," he said. "We proceed on the assumption that your story is true."

"I'll give you another room for the rest of the night," I said. "The guy following you is gone. Lock your door and stay put."

I went up with him to the room.

"That fellow," he said, "Batts."

"Yeah?"

"There are still people like him in the world?"

"Not many," I said. "He's sort of in a class by himself. He's half brain and half heart. The rest is just a shell."

"What time do we leave in the morning?"

"Nine-thirty. I'll call you."

"Look," he said, "about that money."

"Yeah?"

"Marcella gave it to me. She said it was Constancia's. She said it was mine now, but I'd better not let anybody know I had it."

"Then I'm sorry I know."

"I don't care if you know. I just wanted to explain how I got it."

"Okay. Get some sleep."

"Thanks for everything," he said.

I went downstairs.

"Did George Cooler and Amos Bittner take that money to the bank?" I asked.

Jack Pritchard nodded.

"Did they count it?"

"Yes, they did."

"How much was there?"

"Two hundred thousand forty-nine dollars and seventy-one cents."

I went into the suite. Singer Batts had gone back to work on his paper.

CHAPTER III

It was a bright spring day in Chicago. The Midway was green. People were out pushing baby carriages and kids were playing on the lawns.

I found the building where Singer's meeting was and went in with him. It was a kind of club room, cool and dark, with leather chairs and bookcases around the walls. There was a big table in the middle of the room piled with magazines. A lot of nice, quiet-looking guys were sitting around in there and a few women. As soon as Singer walked in, eight or ten of the men jumped up and went to him and he smiled shyly and started shaking hands and mumbling. He was quite a big shot in these circles. Living with him day after day around the Preston Hotel, I would forget about this side of him. I was always a little shocked when I got reminded of it.

It took quite a while for him to break away, but finally he came over to where I was standing by the door.

"I'll take Nick Andrews somewhere," I told him, "and see what develops. One way or another I'll come to Professor Jackson's house this evening before eleven."

"As you wish, Joseph," Singer said.

Nick was lying down on the back seat of the car.

"When did you sleep last before last night?" I asked.

"A couple of days ago. I forget."

I drove to a small tavern on 55th Street and we had some lunch. While we were eating I asked him, "Ever been in Chicago before?"

"Only that one time—the other night."

"You know where Marcella Cipriano works?"

"No. My wife told me, but I forget. In a night club somewhere."

"You better try to get her at home, on the telephone. You don't want to go back there in broad daylight."

"Maybe not."

"Sure not," I said.

He started to get up.

"Wait," I said, "let me call. They might have somebody staked out there."

I went to a telephone booth and found her number in the book. She lived in a fancy apartment house on Delaware. The apartment had a switchboard. The girl said, "Miss Cipriano isn't home. May I take a message?"

"When will she be back?" I asked.

"Not till tomorrow morning," the girl said.

"On the level?" I asked.

The telephone-girl voice faded. She said, "Hell, yes, on the level. Now get off the wire."

I hung up. I went back to the table and told Nick.

"How were you going to go about getting in touch with her?" I asked. "Were you just going to walk up and knock on the door?"

"I hadn't figured that out. The main thing was to get back here."

"Now you're here."

"Now I'm here."

"Where were you going to stay?"

"I don't know that either. Are you acquainted with Chicago?"

"More or less."

"Well, my wife told me that Marcella worked somewhere on the West Side. I thought I'd—"

"It's a big west side."

"It's big all over, but I've got to start somewhere."

He sounded dull, washed-up, as if it didn't really matter anymore whether he did what he set out to do or not. He needed help.

"Later we'll go over on the West Side and see what we can find," I said.

"You've done enough," he said. "I don't want to take your time."

"Today my time is free," I said. "First we'll find a place for you to stay. I know a hotel."

"Let me pay for the lunch."

"You've got a lot of money left?"

"Enough."

"We'll go Dutch."

I paid for mine and he paid for his.

"Let's see what we can find out right now," I said. "Tell me this. Did your wife seem to be very Italian?"

"What do you mean?"

"Did she ever talk about her life in Chicago, about living with Italians?"

"She never talked much about it. She never seemed to be ashamed of being an Italian. She never tried to hide it."

"What was that other name? The name of her first husband?"

"Perotta. Antonio Perotta."

"Did she ever talk about him?"

"Only to tell me he was killed at Anzio."

"Well, he got home before he died."

"Yeah."

I looked up Perotta in the phone book. There were three of them. I called all three. Two answered. One man said he never heard of Antonio Perotta. The other got so excited and his accent was so thick I couldn't understand what he said.

"Let's go to the hotel and get a room," I said. "We can do better from there."

It was out on North LaSalle Street, a workingman's hotel where I had stayed many times. The manager was an old acquaintance, "Big Red" Brooks, a former welterweight boxer. I'd known him for ten years.

He gave the kid a room with a shower on the second floor. I told Nick to lie down for a few minutes and I went downstairs with Big Red.

"The kid's on the lam," he said.

"All right," I said. "But he's not guilty."

"That's the truth, Joe?"

"That's the truth."

"Then okay. What's the trouble?"

I sketched it out for him.

"Had him in a box, eh?" he said.

We sat in Big Red's apartment in the back of the building, drinking beer. Big Red was wide and tall, with sloping shoulders and a bristly beard. The beard was as red as his hair, which was *red*. He was a shrewd guy and a careful one. But once he agreed to stick with you, he stayed stuck. I'd always liked him. Outside of his blown-up ears, there were none of the fighter's marks on him. He spent his spare time reading an encyclopedia. He made notes. He had the biggest fund of useless information of anybody I ever knew.

"He's trying to get in touch with his sister-in-law," I told him. "A girl named Marcella Cipriano."

"It's a big town, Joe."

"I know. But he has to find a place to start from. She works in some West Side joint."

"What kind of a place, Joe?"

"We don't know."

"There couldn't be a good place out there that I know of. What does she do on the side?"

"I don't know that either."

He drank for a while and then he said, "You want to watch your step, Joe. The Italians are a close kind of people. They got a lot of big shots and they don't take nothing from nobody."

"I thought if I could find an Italian taxi driver who lived out in that neighborhood…"

"You are referring to the neighborhood of Milwaukee Avenue and Halstead?"

"That's it."

"I will call Pete London. He knows more cabbies than anybody else in town."

He went to a board hanging on his wall. It had three rows of buzzers with a little name card beside each one and a room number. He punched one of the buzzers, picked up the house telephone and waited.

"Get up and come down, Pete."

We drank some more beer and waited and pretty soon Pete London came into the room, rubbing sleep out of his eyes.

"Sorry to wake you up," I said.

"Pete," Big Red said, "think of the name of some Italian cabby who lives out around Milwaukee Avenue."

"He has to be an Italian?"

"It would be better."

Pete thought it over for a while. Big Red poured him a beer.

"There's Tony Delfino. He lives out there somewhere."

"He work nights or days?"

"Days, the last I heard."

"How could we get hold of him?"

"I think he works out of a stand out there on Halstead. I don't know the number."

"We'll look it up."

"What do you want with an Italian cabby?"

"Information."

Pete shrugged.

"You might get it. Can I go back to bed now? I'll pay the rent next week for sure. Then maybe I'll get some sleep."

Big Red laughed.

"Your credit's all right, Pete. Tony Delfino is this cabby's name?"

"Yeah. I don't know whether he's still working or not."

"Thanks, Pete," I said.

"Okay," he said and went away.

Big Red started looking up numbers and finally found out how to call the cab stand at Halstead near Milwaukee. He rang it up and asked for Delfino. He listened, then hung up.

"He won't come to work till five-thirty."

"I guess the thing to do would be to get out there about that time."

"I guess so. Have another beer, Joe."

"Let me buy you a drink."

"No, Joe. I got it pretty good now. I can afford to serve a little beer."

Pretty soon he said, "I wouldn't just up and start asking questions about this Marcella Cipriano. You don't know who's protecting her."

"I promise you that I'll be careful," I said to him.

We sat there for a while, drinking beer and talking about old times, and about four o'clock I went out to a bar near Michigan and Chicago Avenue, where I knew some people, and at five o'clock I went back to Big Red's place and woke up Nick Andrews.

It was quite an experience. He came up fighting, slipped off the bed and, the first thing I knew, he was climbing out onto the fire escape. I grabbed him and shook him a little and finally he recognized me.

"Sorry," he said. "I was having a dream."

"Feel better now?"

"Yeah. Where are we going?"

"Out to a cab stand, to talk to a guy named Delfino."

"Does he know about Marcella?"

"We don't know. He might. Cab drivers know a lot of people that work in joints."

He washed his face and combed his hair and we got in the car and headed for Halstead and Milwaukee. He didn't say much on the way, except once, when he said, "Why are you doing all this for me? You never saw me until last night."

"I've got nothing else to do," I said.

He kept quiet then.

I parked the car in a lot on Halstead Street and we walked up to the cab stand. There were two cabs and I asked about Delfino.

"He'll be here in a couple of minutes," one of the cabbies said. "He comes on when I go off."

We waited. After about ten minutes another cab drove into the curb and stopped, and the two that had been sitting there drove away. The guy who got out of the new cab had oily black hair that curled up in back under his cap. He was thick and pudgy in front and he wore thick glasses. He waddled across the sidewalk to the phone box, picked it up and talked into it. After a while he hung up and went back to the cab. We were standing there.

"Where to?" he asked, looking at the two of us.

We got in the back seat.

"We want to go to the place where Marcella Cipriano works," I said.

"She don't come to work until—" Then he stopped and looked around at us. "Who?" he said.

"A girl named Marcella Cipriano."

"That's what I thought you said. I don't know her."

"Oh," I said.

He waited.

"This guy is her cousin," I said.

"Yeah. Very interesting," he said.

"He has had an unfortunate experience and he has to get in touch with Marcella."

"I couldn't be of any help."

"All we want to do is talk to her. It's a matter of life or death."

"Sure."

"I'm on the level," I said. "It really is a matter of life or death."

"For who?"

"For two people. Marcella's sister, Constancia, and this kid here, whose name is Nick."

"I'm sorry," he said. "It's also a matter of life or death for me. If I take you to Marcella Cipriano, I wake up tomorrow morning in some alley on my way to purgatory."

"What's wrong with Marcella Cipriano?"

"Nothing. Nothing at all. But I don't know her."

"Put it this way," I said. "You don't have to take us anywhere. We got in here under the mistaken impression that you knew where we could find a couple of girls. You don't. But you can mention the name of a good place to eat and drink in this neighborhood. We especially like Italian food."

He took off his glasses, cleaned them, put them back on, found a cigarette and lit it, squirmed around in his seat, took off and replaced his hat a couple of times and looked up and down the street. Finally he said, "About the best place to eat in this neighborhood is Mother Perri's Pizza Parlor. It's in the book. Now get the hell out of this cab."

"Thank you," I said. "I always forget a face."

"Forget mine," he said.

We went into a drugstore and looked up the address of Mother Perri's Pizza Parlor. It was only two blocks away and we walked over there. It was a small place, with Chianti bottles hanging in rows in the two front windows. Inside, on the counter beside the cash register, was a twenty-six table. Nobody was operating it. It was early for dinner and we went to the back and sat down. There was a small bar back there and a couple of girls sitting at it, sipping long drinks. They were part of the joint. They looked our way and I nodded. They came over to the table and I ordered drinks for the four of us. Nick was uncomfortable.

Halfway through the drink, I said, "When does Marcella come to work?"

"Marcella Cipriano?" one of the girls said.

"Yes."

She looked at her friend. The other girl shook her head slightly.

"I don't know," the first girl said. "I think she's off tonight."

"Thanks," I said. "What does she do? Is she a waitress or is she in the show?"

There was a silence. Then the first girl said, "For your own good, shut up about Marcella Cipriano. Thanks for the drink."

"Have another."

"No thanks."

This was incredible. That they wouldn't let us buy another drink. I began to have the feeling everyone was watching me. I looked around, but couldn't see anybody.

"What's so mysterious?" Nick asked.

"I don't know," I said. "Let's have another drink."

A waiter came and took our order. I wanted it to stretch out as long as possible, so we ordered everything in sight and after a while they began to bring it.

CHAPTER IV

Gradually the place acquired customers: mostly Italian, mostly proletarian and mostly male. The show was a strip routine that would run continuously from seven o'clock.

The bar filled up first, then the tables around us. We sat near a small, cleared area. There was a platform behind it with music stands.

The food was good. It was brought to us by a waitress with long, black hair and a skin like cream. Nick kept staring at her and I had to ask him not to. He was fidgeting all the time.

"Take it easy," I said. "Enjoy the meal."

"Is this all we can do?" he said. "Just sit and wait?"

"It is right now. I've asked too many questions about Marcella already. You'll just have to keep your eyes open till you see her."

As the place filled up, it got noisy. The musicians came in about six-forty-five and tuned up. Then they drifted over to the bar. We ordered more coffee and waited.

At seven o'clock, a door in the rear opened and a tall blonde in a long, white gown came out and walked past us toward the front of the place. Behind her out of the same door came a slight, dark Italian in a tuxedo. He sat down at a table. The musicians went to the stand, picked up their instruments and began to beat out a slow dance tune. The few couples there got up and danced. I kept looking at the slim Italian in the tuxedo. He looked like a movie version of a gigolo. He looked straight ahead and when the waitress came, he didn't even look at her. He just talked to her out of the side of his mouth. I tried to figure out what he was looking at, but I couldn't.

"That's Angelo?" I asked Nick.

Nick said, "Yes."

"We better get out of here."

"He hasn't seen us."

"He might."

"Marcella's up front at that dice table. I didn't say anything before because Angelo was with her."

I excused myself and went to the men's room in the rear. On the way back I looked at the dice table. It was the girl who had come out of the rear door a few minutes earlier. I hadn't been looking for a blonde.

I sat down again.

"We'll wait till the show starts," I said.

A spotlight went on and one of the musicians picked up a microphone.

"The lovely, delightful, entrancing Yvonne," he said. "Come on, Yvonne!"

One of the girls for whom we'd bought a drink came out of the little door into the space. She took the mike and sang a naughty song that didn't hang together very well and then she pushed the mike away and went into the strip routine. It looked as if everybody was watching her. Everybody except Nick, that is.

"Watch her," I said. "The dancer. I'll be right back."

I left the table and worked my way up front to the twenty-six game. Nobody was playing. The blonde sat behind the table and smiled as I came up.

"You don't like the dancers?" she said.

"I'd rather play games," I said.

She handed me the dice box. I rolled a pair of fives and three assorted numbers and held out the fives. I lost and we played again and then again till I was into her for a couple of bucks, and about that time the stripper finished her act and there was some whistling and applause and stamping of feet.

"Marcella—" I said.

"Yes?"

"Marcella Cipriano?"

"Yes. Who are you?"

"I don't matter," I said. "But your brother-in-law—"

"Nick!" she said.

She had leaned forward over the table. I picked up the dice and dropped them into the cup.

"Take it easy," I said. "You told Nick you knew he didn't kill Constancia."

"I know," she said. "Don't talk any more now."

Her face was scared.

The applause died down. I played another game with her and won and then I walked away. As I went back to my table, the slim, dark guy in the tuxedo brushed past me going in the opposite direction. I glanced at him, but he didn't look at me.

He looked like murder on two feet. He was the smoothest, tightest, neatest bundle of vendetta I had ever seen in my life.

I went back to our table. The band played some more and then the second stripper came out. She was more energetic than the first one, but less well-built. I lost interest. Angelo came back, passed our table without looking at us, went behind the bar and picked up a hat and topcoat. He put on the hat and went out through the little rear door. I counted to ten, then decided to play safe and counted some more. Finally I looked around and found Marcella's eye. She nodded once. I got up again and this time Nick went with me. I began to play twenty-six again.

"Nick has to talk to you," I said.

"I can't talk here," she said. "You'll have to come to my place after I get off."

"When?"

"We close at two. You can't come up till three-thirty. My boyfriend takes me home. He'd kill you if he saw you there. He wouldn't understand."

"Angelo?"

"Yes. Come at three-thirty. Ring the bell three times, short. If it's clear, I'll open the door. If not, you'll have to wait."

She was a good-looking girl. The blonde hair wasn't natural, but it was pretty and her face was clear and pale with red lips. She was young. Maybe twenty-two. She sat there behind the dice table, looking at it, not at us, fiddling with her hair.

"Who killed Constancia?" I asked.

She glanced up for a moment, then her eyes flickered away and back to the green felt of the table.

"Later," she said. "Beat it now before Angelo comes back."

"Yes, ma'am," I said.

Nick couldn't seem to think of anything to say. He just stared at Marcella. When I pushed away from the table and started back toward the dining area, he followed me like a kid following his old man. This was what he'd been pushing for, to get to Marcella Cipriano. Now that he'd made it, he didn't have a chance even to talk to her.

"Let's get out of here," I said, motioning to the waitress, who brought a check.

"Shouldn't we wait?" he said. "She said to wait until three-thirty."

"She didn't say to wait right here and I'd rather not. I know a lot of pleasant places in the neighborhood where she lives. We'll go over there."

"I don't know—" he said.

"Come on," I said. "I think Marcella's on the level. And it isn't healthy around here. I can feel it."

"Feel what? I don't feel anything."

"Come on!" I said. "You want a diagram?"

I started out. By the time I got to the front door, he had caught up with me. I didn't look at Marcella as we went out. Whether Nick did or not, I don't know.

Out in the street we walked slowly, breathing the fresh air.

"Dingy places out here," Nick said.

"Yeah. I was in Washington once."

"Well, Washington's not so hot either."

"Chicago could get hot for you right now, if we don't watch out," I said.

"I know."

After a while he said, "Are you sore at me, Joe?"

He was just a kid.

"Hell, no," I said. "I just get that closed-in feeling. I need a lot of fresh air."

We got in the car.

"How old are you, Nick?" I asked.

"I'm old enough," he said.

"When did you enlist?"

"1944."

"You were seventeen then?"

"I—how did you know?"

"It just occurred to me. Then right now you'd be about twenty-three."

"What difference does it make?"

"Nothing. I just wondered."

"You're not so old, for God's sake!"

"No. But I'm fifteen years older than you are and I have spent more than half my life hanging around this town. 'Chi,' we used to call it."

"Well?"

"Well what?"

"What are you trying to say?"

"Only this: I'm a middle-aged man. I don't have the poop a young man has. I found out a long time ago, it's better to wait and lie low and see what develops than it is to go pushing around, trying to make things happen. Because most of the time they happen wrong."

"I don't get it."

"All right. You don't get it. We will now go to Larry White's bar on Chicago Avenue and relax and see what develops. And don't rush me, see? Just don't rush me."

"Anything you say, Joe."

"I know you're anxious to get this thing settled. But we can't settle it without help and it looks to me as if Marcella is our best bet."

"Yeah. If you don't want to hang around, Joe—"

"Sure. I'm getting fascinated. I just don't want to have to move around too much without thinking it over first."

I parked the car and we went into Larry White's place, an intimate little cocktail lounge, with inconspicuous B-girls and well-dressed gentlemen sitting around here and there and a piano player playing softly in a back corner. Larry wasn't in that night, but I knew the piano player and we went back there and bought him a couple of drinks and passed the time of night.

Nick had a hard time to keep from fidgeting. He kept staring around the place and every so often he would signal some waiter and ask him what time it was. The time must have gone very slowly for him. It was only nine-thirty when we went into Larry's.

At ten-thirty I decided I would stick with Nick at least till after we'd seen Marcella, so I called Professor Jackson's house and asked to speak to Singer Batts.

"We've got a warm trail," I said, "and I hate to leave it."

"I will explain to Professor Jackson, Joe."

"Thank you. How did the paper go over?"

"We had a most interesting discussion," Singer said.

"Good. When do you want to start home?"

"No hurry," he said. "I think I'll visit the Newberry Library in the morning."

"Over by Bughouse Square?"

"That's the one."

"Good. I'll pick you up there."

"Very well. Good night, Joseph."

I hung up. I was a little disappointed. I'd hoped he'd ask me how we were making out. But I understood. He wasn't ignoring it. He just doesn't believe in pressing people for information. He likes to get it when it's well done.

Back at the table, Nick said, "Angelo."

"Angelo?" I said.

"That's Marcella's boyfriend."

"Yes. What about him?"

"Do you think he belongs to the Mafia?"

"The what?"

"The Mafia. You know. The Sicilian Union, or whatever it is—"

"I wouldn't know. I'm not a member myself."

"Constancia used to talk about the Mafia."

"Oh?"

"She said her parents lived in fear of the Mafia."

"A lot of people did."

"I guess so… Constancia was a beautiful girl. Sometimes I just can't believe—"

"Come on," I said. "Let's go somewhere else. Ever look at Lake Michigan at night?"

"I never looked at Lake Michigan at all."

"Then you'll see it tonight for the first time."

We went out and got in the car and I drove down to Superior Street and out past the hospital as far as I could go. Then we got out of the car and went across the beach and sat on the pilings there and looked at the lake. I didn't care much about looking at the lake, but right then I didn't know what to do with Nick. We had a long wait ahead of us and we couldn't just sit around and drink for four hours without paying a heavy penalty later. I wanted to be alert when we talked to Marcella.

He was suitably impressed by the black water and the lights stretching from the Planetarium along the South Shore and the other lights here and there. I let him sit there till I thought he couldn't stand it any longer. Then I took him back to the car and we went to a drugstore at the corner of Michigan Boulevard and Chicago Avenue and had hot fudge sundaes and then the drugstore closed and at last it was morning.

"She might have gone home earlier than usual," he said, "since she wanted to talk to us."

"Now listen," I said. "In the first place, she said three-thirty. In the second place, we don't know whether she wants to talk to us or whether she wants us to talk to her. There's a big difference."

"We've got three hours to wait."

"We'll find an all-night movie."

"How will we know what time it is?"

"They all have clocks. Or if you'd feel better, I'll buy a watch."

"All right. Let's go."

Little by little he was tightening up and I was glad to see it. When he had come into the hotel in Preston he was tired and he said a lot of things he wouldn't have said otherwise. Later, after he'd had some sleep, he had become the kid again, following around after his big brother, leaning on me. Now he was beginning to stiffen up. That was good.

I drove down to the Loop and parked and we found a movie that ran all night. We couldn't have made a happier choice. The picture was about the Mafia.

* * * *

We left the theatre at three o'clock and I drove back out to the Near North Side and found a place to park across the street from Marcella's apartment building on Delaware. It was three-twenty when we parked and I made Nick wait.

"All those guns people jump," I said, "they've got hair triggers."

I was certainly full of wisdom that night.

At three-twenty-five the door of Marcella's apartment house opened and a small guy came out and walked to a long, black car. He moved fast and I only caught a glimpse of him. But I saw he was wearing a tuxedo and he was the right size to be Angelo.

"That's him," Nick said.

"All right," I said, "now start counting."

"Counting?"

"Count from one to one hundred. Slow."

"But he's gone now."

"Start counting. Guys like him—they'll maybe drive around the block a couple of times before they get going."

He didn't like it, but he started counting softly under his breath. Every few seconds I would break in to slow him down. It was tough on him. It was tough on me, too, but I'm an older man. I can wait for trouble.

He got through to one hundred and Angelo had not reappeared. I wasn't sure he'd gone yet, but we had to go in sometime.

We crossed the street, walking quietly, and went into the fancy foyer of the apartment building. The inner door was locked. There were rows of buttons under mailboxes, and I found Marcella's apartment number and pushed the button three times.

Nothing happened. I didn't hear the buzzer that unlocked the foyer door. I rang again three times. Nick was standing near the glass door, his hand on the knob. I was worried. If it didn't open in the next few seconds, I could see him going right through the glass.

"Somebody's coming out," he said.

"Good," I said. "Let him open it."

I moved up beside Nick. A big guy with a red face pulled the door open from inside. I pushed it on in and held it open. He looked startled.

"Thanks," I said. "I forgot my key and I guess my wife's sound asleep."

He walked on past us and went outside.

Marcella's apartment was halfway down the hall on the north side of the fifth floor. We walked down there and I knocked on the door.

Nobody came. I tried the knob but the door was locked. I knocked again. Still no answer.

"Maybe there's a back door," Nick said.

"Maybe. But why doesn't she come? We didn't see her leave the building."

He started off down the corridor toward the rear of the building. At the back there was an intersecting corridor. We turned right and found another door and a back stairs. The door looked as if it would be the back door of Marcella Cipriano's apartment.

I knocked on it. Again nobody came and I tried the knob. The door opened.

"Should we go in?" Nick asked.

"I think we should," I said. "Even if nobody's home."

Nobody was home in the kitchen, all steel and chrome, built for maximum efficiency in minimum space. Everything was built into the walls and all the doors were sliding. There were no dirty dishes in the sink.

A swinging door led into a combination dinette and living room, furnished moderne extreme.

There were no dirty dishes in here either, but there was plenty of everything else, all over the room. A lamp was burning in one corner and it showed us sheer havoc. All the drawers in all the tables that had drawers were pulled out and lying on the floor. What had been in the drawers was dumped in piles. Papers, letters, playing cards, dice, matches, cigarettes, address books. You couldn't take a step without walking on some litter. The cushions in the davenport had been slit with a knife and the stuffing half-pulled out of them. Same with the upholstery on the chairs. The thick rug had been pulled up and hauled into a pile in one corner. The framed pictures on the walls were hanging crooked.

"What happened?" Nick asked.

"I don't know," I said. "We'll look in the bedroom."

We went through a little hallway past the bathroom. It was tile and chrome and spotless. Nothing was disturbed in there, probably because there wasn't anything that could be disturbed.

The bedroom was the same as the living room: littered up and cut to ribbons. Mattress, pillows, bedclothes were twisted and cut. Dresser drawers had been pulled out and dumped.

Nick started across the room, tripped over a drawer and fell down. The door of a clothes closet in the far corner of the room swung open slowly.

And that's how we found Marcella Cipriano, hanging from a hook in her own closet.

Nick saw her when he started to get up, untangling himself from a rumpled sheet. He made a funny kind of gurgling sound in his throat and I saw his mouth working. Finally he got some words out.

"Joe—I—my God!" he said.

"Yeah," I said. "Take it easy."

I went over to the closet.

She was wearing the same white gown she had worn at Mother Perri's place. Her blonde hair was rumpled and tumbled about her face and neck. There was a rope, a length of clothes line, twisted around her neck and knotted in back. The other end of the rope was tied to a clothes hook high on the wall. Her feet touched the floor. Her knees were slightly bent and she sagged backward against the wall.

I touched her face. It was not cold or stiff.

"Come here," I said and Nick started toward me.

I got my arms around her waist and lifted her until the rope came slack. "Loosen the knot," I said.

He hesitated. I couldn't blame him.

I held her against the wall with one arm and got my other hand free. I found her wrist and felt for a pulse. There wasn't any. I put my face against her partly-open mouth and held my breath. I didn't feel hers. I felt below her left breast toward the center and felt no heartbeat. Her eyes were nearly closed. I lifted one lid and looked into her eye. The pupil had already begun to lose its shape. She was dead.

I let her down gently until the rope went taut again.

"Shouldn't we—" Nick said and his voice stuck in his throat. "Shouldn't we take her down?"

"Not if she's dead. And she's dead."

He didn't want to look at her any more. He turned around and walked away from the closet. I followed him.

"All right, Nicky boy," I said, "get going."

He stared at me.

"Get—going?"

"Get. Go down the back stairs and out the back door. Go through the alley to Chicago Avenue and turn to the right. Go back to LaSalle Street and Big Red's hotel and up to your room and go to bed. Just go to bed and stay there till you hear from me."

"But, Joe—"

"Shut up," I said. "What did you run away from before?"

"I know, but—"

"If you get caught here, you're cooked, sonny. Get going now."

"What are you going to do?"

"After you go I'm going to count to one hundred. Then I'm going to call the cops. I'm going to suggest to the cops that they start looking for Angelo."

I found a cigarette in my pocket and lit it.

"And after that," I said, "I'm going to call Singer Batts."

He looked at me for a moment, then turned and went out of the room. I heard the door close softly out back and I guessed he was going down the back steps. I hoped he'd make it. I began to count to one hundred.

CHAPTER V

But after I called the cops, I decided not to make another call through the apartment switchboard to Singer Batts. I could check with him later. In the meantime, I had to think up something to tell the cops. I was in it real good now. I could have walked out and left the place, if it hadn't been for Nick. I'd led him in and I felt as if I had to lead him out. I hoped it wouldn't take too much time.

I was sitting on the torn-up sofa, thinking about it, when the door opened and this maid came in.

She opened the door slowly and peeked around the edge of it like a chambermaid in a fancy hotel. Then she came on into the room. She had a dust mop with her, a broom, a dustpan and outside in the corridor I saw a vacuum cleaner. She wore a long, shapeless, gray skirt, a dirty white blouse and a sweater. There was a white cap on her head. A few hairs stuck out below the cap. They weren't gray. Her face was flat, without make-up, the eyes colorless and the cheeks white. Her lips had no rouge on them. But her face wasn't old.

She came on into the room, dragging the vacuum cleaner in from the corridor.

"Just cleanin' up," she said, staring at me.

"Late, isn't it?" I said.

"Miss Cipriano works nights," she said. "I always clean her apartment at this time."

"Oh. Well, she won't be working nights any more."

She stared at me some more.

"What do you mean, sir?" she said.

"Look in the bedroom," I said.

She went through the little hall past the bathroom and into the bedroom. She was gone for quite a while. She was gone for so long I wondered what had happened to her and I got up and started in there. She met me coming back through the hall.

"She's dead?" she said.

"She's dead."

"Why would she want to do a thing like that?"

"I do not know," I said.

"I'd better start cleaning the place up," she said.

I looked at the litter all over everywhere.

"Where are you going to start?"

She looked around too.

"I don't know. Somebody has to," she said.

"When do you really clean this apartment?" I asked.

"What was that?"

"Go ahead," I said. "To hell with it. The cops will be here in a couple of minutes. You won't have time after that."

"The cops?"

Her face looked interested suddenly. Some of the flatness went out of it.

"Yeah," I said. "Naturally. The cops. Who else?"

"I wouldn't want to be here when the police came," she said.

"Then you better get out now," I said.

"Yes, I guess so," she said.

She picked up her things and went out, looking around the room as she went. Hopelessly. After she'd gone I kept remembering her. She was cool. She was young. She was dressed like a maid. But she didn't talk like a maid. She didn't act like a maid.

If she was a maid, I was Joe DiMaggio.

When the cops came, I was sitting on the edge of the ruined davenport, smoking my sixth cigarette. The cops were a lieutenant, a sergeant and two boys in uniform. The lieutenant was an old, tired guy who would retire in another couple of years. He talked to me like a father.

"Now, son," he said, "what were you doing here in this girl's apartment?"

I had thought it over and made up my mind. It wasn't good, but it was the best we had.

"I met her in a joint, where she worked," I said, "and I made a date with her. I came up and found her like this."

"Where does she work?"

"Mother Perri's Pizza Parlor. I don't think she'll get to work on time tomorrow."

"Mother Perri's Pizza Parlor," he said, writing laboriously into his little notebook. "Dice girl?"

"Yes," I said.

"You made a date with her for three o'clock in the morning?"

"Three-thirty," I said.

"Kind of late, isn't it, for a date?"

"She had to wait for her boyfriend to leave."

"Steady boyfriend?"

"I guess so."

"What would his name be?"

"His first name is Angelo. He's small and dark and I saw him go out of here about three-twenty-five."

"Wait a minute," he said, and wrote some more in his book, wetting the pencil every now and then with his tongue.

"What's your name, son?"

"Joe."

"Joe what?"

"Joe Spinder."

"You from out of town?"

"Way out." I told him the name.

"Just come up to the city to raise some hell, eh?"

He tore a page out of his notebook and handed it to the sergeant. The sergeant looked at it, went to the telephone and started dialing numbers. The lieutenant got up stiffly and went into the bedroom. I followed him. The two boys in uniform had taken Marcella Cipriano's picture from as many different angles as they could figure out, and after they finished they took her down off the hook and stretched her out on the bed. One of them was cutting the rope away from her neck. I leaned over and took a look. The rope had been tied behind her neck with a square knot. There was a faint bluish groove high up under her chin where the rope had cut in. There were no bruises or broken blood vessels along the edges of the groove.

The lieutenant watched me staring at her.

"You interested in crime detection?" he asked.

"Not especially."

"Then what are you staring at?"

"I was just wondering how she managed to tie that knot so tight."

He just looked at me.

"Call the coroner's office," he said and one of the boys went out to the other room.

The lieutenant looked around the room.

"It was messed up like this when you came in?" he said.

"Yes," I said.

"How did you get in?"

I told him.

"Why didn't you go away when she didn't answer the front door?"

"I thought something might be wrong. I had seen the boyfriend go out but I hadn't seen her go out."

"Maybe she didn't want to see you."

"Maybe not, in her condition," I said.

He grunted. The sergeant called from the other room and the lieutenant went out. I stood and looked at Marcella Cipriano on the bed and I felt bad. She was a good-looking girl. It was a shame to see her so dead and finished. Also, she was the only link for Nick between his wife's murder and whoever had done it. But mostly it bothered me because she had been so beautiful and so young and now she was nothing.

The lieutenant called me and I went back to the living room.

"Sit down," he said.

I sat.

"Have a cigarette."

He held the match for me, blew it out.

"Who was the guy with you at Mother Perri's?" he asked.

He was very sharp. He whipped that one in very fast, very neat and he caught me on my heels.

"What guy?" I said, which was wrong.

"Go ahead, smoke the cigarette," he said.

Pretty soon he said, "There was a guy with you. A younger kid."

"Oh, yeah," I said brightly. "I ran into him somewhere last night. We hit a few spots. I left him later."

"You left him where?"

"At an all-night movie down in the Loop."

"What movie?"

I told him. I thought the girl in the box office would remember us going in, but that nobody would have noticed us coming out. I hoped.

"Why did you leave him?"

"I had this date."

"Where did you pick him up?"

I rubbed my head.

"I don't remember. Some bar."

"Try to remember."

"I'll try."

It was not going good at all now. I hated this guy. I knew guys who would cover for me, but only if I could get to them first. And I didn't see how I could.

The door opened and the coroner's men came in. The lieutenant told me to stay where I was and led the coroner's lads back to the bedroom.

I sat on the davenport and finished the cigarette. The sergeant stood in the doorway to the bedroom and looked at me. Pretty soon the lieutenant pushed past him and came into the living room.

"Let's go," he said.

"Where?"

"Where we can talk some more," he said.

The sergeant moved in beside me and the lieutenant went out into the corridor. The three of us walked down to the elevator and the lieutenant pushed the button and we waited. Nobody said anything.

We went out to the street and the lieutenant opened the back door of a squad car parked at the curb.

"Can I lock my car?" I asked him.

"You got anybody you can send for it?" he asked.

"Not till morning."

"Morning's all right. Go lock it."

The sergeant went across the street with me and I locked my car doors. Then we went back and I climbed into the back seat of the squad car with the lieutenant and we started up, heading for the Loop.

The silence sat there around us like a flock of vultures and I decided to let it sit. I thought, how does a guy let himself get into these things? For a stranger, a kid, from another city. Because his wife got murdered and then his wife's sister and I happened to come along in between.

Suddenly I was sleepy. I leaned my head against the back of the seat and the next thing I knew the lieutenant was shaking me and we were going into a big, gloomy, official-looking building, which was evidently the back entrance of City Hall, and we went up a flight of wide wooden stairs into a bare, dimly lighted office with steel filing cases against the walls and a battered desk near a big window.

The sergeant closed the blinds on the window and turned on an over-head light. It was a bright light and I blinked under it.

"Sit down," the lieutenant said.

I sat down.

"Cigarette?" he said, holding one out.

"Thanks," I said. "I got some out of my car."

I opened the fresh pack, got out a cigarette and lit it. The sergeant sat down on the edge of the lieutenant's desk. The lieutenant sat down behind the desk and stared at me.

"Why did you do it?" he said.

"Do what?"

"Why did you kill her?"

"I didn't," I said. "Everything was exactly like I told you."

He sighed.

Just keep quiet, I kept telling myself. Just let them talk. Just hold on. If you're innocent, you're safe.

Sure. Safe.

The telephone rang. The lieutenant looked at it. He let it ring three or four times and finally he picked it up.

"Lieutenant Morgan," he said.

He listened for a while. Then he said, "That's ridiculous."

He listened some more.

"It don't make sense," he said.

He listened a long time this next session. His heavy, weather-beaten face was impassive.

"Oh," he said finally, "whatever you say."

He hung up. The door of the office opened and a guy came in. He was short and fat and genial-looking. He wore thick glasses. He had gray hair fringing a bald skull. He looked so happy he was bursting with it.

"Hi, Lieutenant," he said. "You've got a boy here, named—" he looked at a paper he was carrying, "—Joe Spinder?" He pronounced it wrong, making the *i* long.

The lieutenant grunted. The fat guy threw the paper on the desk.

"I'll take him along with me," he said.

The lieutenant shrugged.

"You can keep the paper," he said. "We're not holding him."

"Oh, I'm sure of that, Lieutenant," the fat guy said. "But would you mind telling me why?"

"Sure, I'd mind," the lieutenant said. "Get the hell out of here."

"I understood there'd been a homicide."

"You misunderstood," the lieutenant said. "Now get out."

He threw the writ on the floor and slammed a drawer shut in his desk. The fat guy grinned at me and held out his arm.

"Come along, son," he said.

I got up.

"Who are you?" I asked. "If you're an attorney—"

"Don't worry, son," he said, laughing. "No charge by the police—no charge by Honest Abe Glass. Just want to talk to you."

"Watch it, son," the lieutenant said to me. "He'll talk you right out of your pants."

"Now, Lieutenant," Honest Abe said.

He held the door open for me and we walked out into the hall and down the steps to the back of the building. There was a car parked there by the door. This Glass opened the door. In the back seat was a thickset, not bad-looking guy with a scar across his chin.

"Well, Mr. Whitney!" I said.

He didn't answer. The door slammed shut behind me and I sat down. I didn't have much choice.

Glass went around and climbed into the front seat beside the driver. The car started up. Glass looked back at Whitney.

"I didn't have to spring him," he said. "They let him go."

"Why?" Whitney asked.

"I don't know," Glass said. "Said there wasn't any homicide."

The driver got the car onto Michigan and went very fast out past Chicago Avenue and turned west on Oak Street. He stopped in front of a second-class apartment building, three stories high, and Whitney got out and held the car door for me. I climbed out.

"Come inside," he said, starting toward the front door of the building.

"No," I said. "My car's parked around the corner. I'm going home and get some sleep. Thanks for the lift."

The guy who had driven the car stepped in behind me. He shoved something small and round into my kidneys.

"Move," he said, with a thick accent. "Inside."

That was different.

I followed Whitney inside the building and up to the second floor. He opened a door with a key and we went into a small apartment, conventionally and cheaply furnished. Whitney switched on a floor lamp and closed the Venetian blinds. The driver stood away from me, still holding the gun. I noticed Glass hadn't come up with us.

"Max," Whitney said, "put the gun away."

The guy dropped the gun into his pocket.

I looked at this Max. He looked like his accent—squat and heavy with a butch haircut and no neck. His skin was dark, with white splotches here and there. He looked as if he had got out of Germany before the military boys could nab him. He looked as if he should have hung alongside Mussolini—in the same position.

Looking at Whitney for the second time, away from my home grounds, I thought he didn't look so good. He was well-built and not bad in the face, but there was something wrong. His eyes were crooked—not cross-eyed exactly, but flat and dull and not quite level. The scar on his chin didn't help any.

"Where's Nick Andrews?" he asked.

"I don't know," I said. "We went to an all-night movie. I left him downtown."

"You're lying," he said. "Where is he?"

"The hell with it," I said.

Max stepped up and hit me in the mouth. I tasted the blood. I was sore enough now to fight, but I knew it would be ridiculous. At least one of them had a gun and they were both heavier and deadlier than I.

"Where is he?" Whitney asked.

"What do you want with him?" I asked.

"I want to turn him in, where he belongs."

"To take the heat off who?" I asked, guessing.

Max hit me again. I tried to roll away from it, but it had come too fast. My lip was bleeding in two places now.

I figured fast. I couldn't depend on it for sure—but it might work—it just might—"All right," I said, giving in. "He's nothing to me. I'll take you to him."

"Just tell us where he is," Whitney said, grinding his teeth a little.

"It wouldn't help you any," I said. "Where he is, you couldn't get to him."

"All right then. You take us."

Max opened the door. I walked out into the hall, and they followed me. We went downstairs and got in that car again. The attorney, Glass, was gone.

"How'd you know I'd been pinched?" I asked.

Whitney just grunted.

"Where to?" Max asked with his accent.

"South Side," I said. I gave him Professor Jackson's address on University Avenue.

Whitney looked hard at me. "This is the right place?"

"It's the right place."

Max got going. He didn't waste any time.

Twenty minutes later we turned out of Jackson Park, and Max found University and pulled up in front of Professor Jackson's house. It was dark and quiet along the street, a respectable, very learned street, housing a lot of smart, quiet people.

We went up to the door. I noticed there was a light burning far in the back, in the professor's study. It wasn't unusual for Singer and the professor to sit up all night, talking. That was good. It meant I wouldn't have to wake anybody up.

I rang the bell and waited. Pretty soon I saw a new light go on and Singer Batts came shambling along through the living room to the door. That was good too, if he was as fast at mind reading as he usually is.

He opened the door.

"Joseph," he said quietly.

He looked at Whitney and at Max. He looked at me and I concentrated.

"They want Nick," I said. "I guess we might as well give up."

There was a pause while he studied my face. Then he nodded once.

"Very well," he said, backing away from the door. "Won't you come in?"

I stepped inside and Whitney and Max stepped in behind me. Singer shuffled away toward the back of the house.

"I'll have to wake him," he said. "He's very tired."

"No tricks," Whitney muttered in my ear.

I didn't answer.

We stood in the living room near the door, waiting. I began to count. There's nothing like counting to keep yourself under control.

I got up to seventy-five. Then the shuffling steps came back. Two sets this time. Singer came first and Professor Jackson was right behind him. Professor Jackson was a tall, gray-haired man, very distinguished-looking, wearing a pince-nez. He was wearing bedroom slippers and a smoking jacket. His eyes were bright behind the glasses. In his arms he carried the biggest shotgun I have ever seen, before or since. He pointed it at Whitney.

"Put your hands up," Singer said quietly.

Whitney began to swear softly, using the biggest possible vocabulary.

"Here, here!" Professor Jackson said. "That's no way to talk."

Whitney kept it up.

"Perhaps they have guns," Singer said to me.

I found the one in Max's pocket and went over him for more. There weren't any more. I went over Whitney and found a .38 in a shoulder holster. He glared at me, his mouth working. I couldn't figure him out. He couldn't be that dumb—to get the wrong suitcase, and then to let himself be led into a set-up like this. Maybe he had just been over-confident.

"Now you may go," Singer said.

"You're making a mistake," Whitney said, trying to sound reasonable and controlled. "It's a serious offense to conspire with a murderer."

"I'm sure it is," Singer said. "It's very late. Will you please go now?"

"Out, out!" I said, making a sweeping motion with my arm.

They glared at me for a couple of seconds, and then they walked out. I closed the door behind them.

"They might come back with another gun," I said.

"That would be ill-advised," Singer said. "Professor Jackson's gun is loaded."

Professor Jackson glanced down absent-mindedly.

"So it is," he said. "Don't know that I could shoot a man down though, if my life depended on it. Just not made that way."

"Joseph," Singer said, "what happened? Your mouth is swollen."

"It's pretty late," I said. "I'll tell you, if you want to listen."

"By all means," Professor Jackson said. "It's not often we scholars run into such stimulating circumstances. Here Singer and I have been discussing things that happened three hundred years ago in Elizabethan England, and you've been out mixing with quite another element."

"Yes, Professor," I said. "Quite an element."

We went back into the professor's study and sat down. Singer brought me a glass of cold milk. It tasted good.

CHAPTER VI

After I'd finished my story, Singer sat with his eyes closed, leaning back in a high wing chair. Professor Jackson got up, went to a cupboard, got down a bottle and poured himself a small measure of brandy. He poured some for me too.

"My word!" he said. "You have been busy, haven't you?"

It was nearly six o'clock in the morning. I was so sleepy I could neither keep my eyes open nor my mouth shut. But I kept thinking of Nick, knowing we had to get back to him, even if only for a few minutes. The tough guy, Whitney, surely wouldn't stop looking for him.

It was Singer who suggested I go to bed. I was glad to. He led me upstairs to Professor Jackson's guest room and I undressed and turned in.

"We'll have to see Nick again before we leave," I said.

"We'll talk about it when you wake up," he said.

I turned over and went to sleep. I think I turned over. I remember starting to do it. I don't remember completing the turn.

I slept for about four hours, until ten o'clock. When I woke up, Singer Batts was sitting in a chair by the bedroom window with the morning paper on his lap. He handed it to me. I hiked myself up in the bed and read the story on the front page.

"DICE GIRL IN SUICIDE," it said.

It was a very short story. It told how Lieutenant Morgan had investigated the scene, found Marcella Cipriano hanging in her closet and questioned a man from out of town who was there when the police arrived. It told my story the way I had told it to the lieutenant, without reference to anybody else who might have been with me during the evening. It was also without reference to Angelo. As far as the police were concerned, the case was closed. Suicide.

This was very well from Nick's standpoint, and from mine, and probably from Angelo's. It didn't explain why Marcella Cipriano had made a shambles out of her own apartment before she hung herself. The shambles wasn't mentioned in the paper.

I looked at Singer. He didn't look happy. He had a hunch that once more he was up to his neck in foul play. He didn't like it. He never liked it—not in any case we ever worked on.

But, being the kind of guy he was, he would be thinking about Nick Andrews too. He couldn't help it.

He glanced at me.

"I am trying to remember what you told us earlier," he said. "The girl's feet were on the floor and the rope was knotted in back of her neck with a square knot. What kind of hook had been used as a scaffold?"

"One of those ordinary wire hooks with a long loop up above and a shorter, circular one underneath. The kind that screws into the wall."

"Not a strong support," he said. "Great care would have to be exercised in lowering oneself from such a gibbet. The hook could be expected to pull out."

"Yeah," I said.

"It would be extremely difficult to accomplish such a maneuver after death."

I looked at him.

"Somebody helped her," I said.

"Undoubtedly."

"Her neck wasn't broken," I said. "There weren't any bruises on it."

"I suppose it is our civic duty," he said, "to suggest to the Chicago police that in view of the evidence and the circumstance that this young lady's sister was destroyed barely two days ago in the same apartment, the verdict of suicide is unlikely."

"I suppose so," I said. "But what about Nick?"

"I am thinking about that."

He thought about it for a while and then he said, "Refresh my memory, Joseph. You found a suitcase full of currency in Nick's possession?"

"In Preston, yeah, I did."

"He made no explanation of that?"

"Nothing except that his sister-in-law, Marcella, had given it to him."

He thought some more and finally he said, "Call your friend, Lieutenant Morgan, on the telephone. I think that is as far as we need to go. Nothing need be said about Nick."

"I'd rather you called him."

"But he doesn't know me, Joseph. He knows you."

"All right. But stand by."

I got up and dressed and we went downstairs. Mrs. Jackson had some breakfast waiting for us—hot muffins, eggs and bacon and coffee. The professor was still asleep. Mrs. Jackson was about to go shopping and she said goodbye and went away. We ate some breakfast.

After that we went into the study and I put in a call to Lieutenant Morgan's office. Singer stood beside me, stooped in the shoulders, his long neck twisted as he bent his head to hear what I would say.

Finally Lieutenant Morgan came on. He sounded tired and fed-up. He remembered me.

"The girl couldn't have committed suicide," I said.

"You don't say," he said.

I outlined the main facts. When I finished, the lieutenant said, "That's all now?"

"That isn't enough?" I said.

"Afraid not, sonny. The coroner's office made a thorough investigation. The case is closed. Don't lose yourself any sleep over it."

"Did you find Angelo?" I asked.

"Angelo?"

"The boyfriend."

"I don't seem to remember anything about Angelo."

"Oh. Well, you knew, of course, that Marcella Cipriano's sister, Constancia, was murdered in the same place only the day before yesterday."

There was a pause.

"No, sonny," the lieutenant said, "I didn't know that. But I don't think it enters into this, does it? Thanks for trying to help."

He hung up. I hung up, too, and looked at Singer.

"Somebody wants it should be a suicide and that everybody should forget about it."

"Indeed," Singer said.

I went and got some more coffee.

"She was a beautiful girl, this Marcella."

"No doubt," Singer said.

"Kind of tough on Nick. He can't run forever. They'll find him."

"I imagine they will." He was staring moodily through the window.

"If somebody could find out who killed Marcella Cipriano, they might find out who killed Nick's wife, too. That would fix things up for Nick. He's a good kid," I said.

"I liked him very much." Singer sighed heavily. He got up and paced around for a while. Then he said, "All right. We'll go back and see Nick."

He wrote a note to Professor Jackson. We left the house and went to the Illinois Central Station at 59th Street and started downtown.

Singer made me go over the details of the thing again and when I finished we were at Randolph and Michigan, looking for a cab.

We got a cab that took us to where my car was parked on Delaware. We got in my car and drove to Big Red's hotel. We went up to Nick's room.

Nick wasn't there. The bed had been slept in. His hat was hanging on a chair in the corner. There was the smell of occupancy, the smell you learn to recognize. But Nick was gone.

There were no signs of a struggle. Only the mussed-up bed and the smell were evidence that anybody had been in the room at all.

Then Singer leaned down, reached part way under the bed and came up with a piece of paper, maybe six inches square. He handed it to me. It was blank on one side, and I turned it over. On the other side was the imprint of a human hand, in black ink. I looked at it and then I looked at Singer and crumpled the paper in my hand, throwing it on the floor.

"Oh, my God," I said. "That old stuff."

Singer sat down on the edge of the bed. He wasn't thinking about any "old stuff" business. He was very serious. He sat for a long time, his head pulled down into his coat collar like a turtle's head, his long hands quiet in his lap, his face miserable. After a while he looked up at me and spread his hands.

"To think that I, a quiet, unassuming, bashful exponent of Shakespearean scholarship, a small-town man with a small-town mind, should continually find myself in these distressing and morbid situations—to think that I am unable to summon the moral courage to say, 'This is not my affair.'"

"You can say it for all of me."

He studied me. He studies everything.

"Can I, Joseph?"

"Sure. Except—she was a beautiful girl, that Marcella Cipriano. She was a honey. And this Nick—he's just a kid."

"Just a kid," Singer said.

"But it's no skin off our backs."

"Crudely stated, but true, in a way."

"What do we do?"

He hadn't planned it this way. He had planned a quiet evening's discussion with Professor Jackson, a leisurely morning at Newberry Library, a leisurely drive back home and the peace and quiet of our suite in the Preston Hotel.

But there was Nick. And everything was foul about this business. It would either be cleared up, or it would be left to hang there in Singer's memory. And if it hung there in his memory, like the decayed corpse of a hanged man—or woman—there would be no peace in the quiet suite of the Preston Hotel. Not for him and not for me.

"What do we do?" I asked again.

"We find Nick," he said.

"It's a big town," I said.

"It won't be hard to find Nick. It's what comes afterward that will give us difficulty."

We went downstairs to Big Red's apartment on the first floor. He greeted Singer like a long-lost brother. He loved to get Singer into conversations. He picked up a lot of information that way. He had a section in his notebook headed "Singer Batts." Damnedest notebook you ever saw. Full of facts and obscure quotations. If he lived long enough, he'd have every encyclopedia on the market backed right off the map.

"I have a small seed to plant," Singer said. "I am inserting an advertisement in the personal column of the afternoon papers. It will probably result in some visitors asking to see Nick Andrews. I want you to talk to them long enough to get me a description, and then tell them Nick has moved out."

Big Red nodded happily.

"Sure, Singer," he said. "Be glad to. What kind of people will they be?"

"I am not sure. They may be somewhat rough and ready."

Big Red flexed his big hands. "One reason I'm successful in the hotel business," he said, "—I don't take no nonsense."

"I'm sure you don't," Singer said. "Now, tell me—on whom should I call to discuss a matter of interest to the Italian-American population of this city?"

"You want the big shot, or just somebody down the line?" Big Red asked.

"The big shot, if you please," Singer said.

Big Red looked worried. "Caesar Fortunata," he said. "But be careful, Singer. Be mighty careful."

"Yes," Singer said. "I think Mr. Fortunata will understand that I am with him, not against him."

"I hope so," Big Red said. "I hope he understands that."

We walked away. There was a cold lump in the pit of my stomach.

"Fortunata?" I said to Singer. "He's big. He's international."

"True, Joseph. Our reception will depend on one thing."

"Yeah?" I said. "What thing?"

"It will depend on whether Marcella Cipriano was murdered by an Italian or by somebody else—anybody else."

"Remember the Angelo," I said.

"I will remember."

We went across the street to a drugstore and Singer telephoned an ad to the classified section of two evening papers. One of them would be out after dinner.

The ad read: "I have the money. Let's make a deal. N. A."

The first little piece of the puzzle dropped into place. The lump in my stomach got colder.

CHAPTER VII

Caesar Fortunata lived in a penthouse on the North Side. He was practically a myth. Untouchable, rich like a maharajah, he was a top boy in the American division of the international underworld. I had heard of him and I knew Singer had too. But it would never have occurred to me to call on him for any reason I could think of. He was so big he didn't have to dirty his hands any more. All his work was done for him.

The penthouse was quite a thing. The public elevator only went to the last floor below it. We had to walk up the back stairs and there we found ourselves in a blind alley with an iron grille between the top of the stairs and the corridor leading to the penthouse door. A guy sat at a desk behind the grille. He was a busy little man with a pencil stuck behind his ear, a switchboard in front of him and a big pad of paper on the desk. He peered at us.

"Mr. Fortunata," Singer said.

"Your name?" the guy said.

"Singer Batts."

"Spelling?"

Singer spelled it for him and he looked at me.

"Joe Spinder."

"Spelling?"

We went through it again. He looked at his wrist watch and made a note beside our names. Then he turned around and waved his arm. A big ape of a man came along the corridor, looked at us through the grille, reached for a buzzer. The grille swung open and the big one stepped out. The grille closed behind him.

"Hold up your arms," he said.

We did it. He went over us with his hands, swiftly, with skill. It took him about thirty seconds. Then he stepped back.

"All right, Eddie," he said and the buzzer rang again.

The grille swung open and we stepped through into the corridor. The ape stepped in after us and the grille closed. He pointed down the corridor.

"Third door on the left down the hall," he said. "Ring the bell."

But what if Marcella was killed by an Italian, I kept thinking, as we walked down the hall. What if Mr. Fortunata finds us too curious?

Singer rang the bell. The door opened right away and we were looking at a small Filipino in a white coat. His face was blank. His eyes traveled over Singer, standing there tall and scrawny in his forty-five-dollar chain store suit that didn't fit him anywhere and his scuffed shoes and the green shirt with the too-big collar. Through the blankness, you could see the houseboy was thinking about the strange people who came to see Mr. Fortunata.

"What is it?" he said.

"We wish to speak with Mr. Fortunata," Singer said.

"Mr. Fortunata is not in."

"Then we will wait."

"Mr. Fortunata will not be in for a long time. Maybe two, three week."

"We will wait," Singer said.

This threw the little guy off some. He lifted what he had in the way of eyebrows.

"Two, three week you wait?" he asked.

"If necessary," Singer said. "I wish to see Mr. Fortunata about an urgent matter."

"What matter?"

"The matter of the murder—" Singer said, and paused, "of Marcella Cipriano."

The blankness came back into the face.

"Marcella Cipriano," he repeated. "Wait here."

He closed the door. This is it, I thought. This will tell us the story. Mr. Fortunata will probably see us. The question is, will we see him first?

We waited about five minutes. Then the door opened again and the Filipino nodded his head and stood out of the way.

We walked into a dimly-lighted reception hall, large for an apartment, even a penthouse. Paintings hung on the walls, each one with a little light on it, as in a museum. Singer looked at them.

"My word!" he said softly. "These are priceless."

"Yeah," I said.

The Filipino walked across the reception hall to a wide door with a Chinese design painted on it in red lacquer. He knocked twice on the door and a voice from inside said something I didn't catch. The Filipino opened the door and nodded at us again. We walked over there and through the door and it closed behind us.

Caesar Fortunata was sitting at a small desk in a corner of the room. He wore a black dressing gown with white dragons on the back, a black scarf around his neck and black, patent leather slippers with heels. He was examining a green vase, turning it this way and that, holding it up to the light. His hair was gray and long, combed carefully back and curling above the ears.

We stood and waited and after a while he set the vase down on the desk, turned slowly in his chair and looked at us. He had a dried-up old face, heavily wrinkled. He smiled a little, showing white teeth, and the smile was not unfriendly, but it stopped with the mouth. His eyes were like two chrome-plated buttons.

"Sit down, gentlemen," he said.

We found chairs and sat in them. Caesar Fortunata got up, walked across the room and sat down in a big leather chair near Singer. He bent his head a little, turning it so that his left ear pointed toward Singer, as if he were deaf in the other one.

"You wished to mention the death of Marcella Cipriano," he said.

"Yes," Singer said.

"I understood by the papers," Fortunata said, "that Miss Cipriano committed suicide. A tragic circumstance."

"Very," Singer said. "But it was not suicide."

Fortunata smiled again and spread his hands. The full sleeves of his dressing gown fell away. He had long, thin hands, carefully manicured.

"Gentlemen," he said, "now you come here and tell me that Marcella Cipriano did not commit suicide. Forgive me. I don't understand. I have read the newspapers."

It was a good act, well performed.

"I too read the newspapers," Singer said. "But in addition, I have gathered some other information. Marcella Cipriano was murdered."

"Indeed?"

He shifted his eyes from Singer to me.

"You, perhaps, would be the young man who was at the scene of the tragedy, the one mentioned in the papers?"

"Yeah," I said.

"I see," Fortunata said. "But you did not murder Marcella Cipriano?"

"No."

"And you don't know who did?"

"No."

He looked at Singer again.

"But you are certain she was murdered."

"Quite certain."

"Tell me why you think so."

He settled back in his chair. Singer told him about the evidence that pointed to murder. He did not mention Nick Andrews. He stuck to the physical evidence. When he finished, Fortunata looked at his nails, adjusted the sleeves of his dressing gown and laid his hands flat on the arms of his chair.

"You are a clever man, Mr.—"

"Batts. Singer Batts."

"Singer Batts. That is an English name?"

"Yes."

"That is what I thought. Tell me, Mr. Batts—how do you account for the reluctance of the police to reopen the investigation into Marcella Cipriano's—death?"

"I don't account for it," Singer said. "I came here because I assumed you would be interested in the death by violence of one of your countrymen."

There was a pause while Fortunata surveyed us. His chrome-plated eyes glittered a little in his wrinkled face.

"But I am very much interested," he said finally. "Yes, Mr. Batts, I am interested. And I am not alone in my interest."

He reached up behind his shoulder and pulled a long bell cord hanging against the wall. I didn't hear anything ring. A door opened at the opposite end of the room and a man stepped through it. He paused for a moment, then came across to where I was sitting. He came very close, and suddenly I was sitting straight and stiff in my chair and his knife was lying alongside my throat, right where it would bleed the most if it got cut. He had come so fast I hadn't had time to look at his face. But it didn't require much looking to recognize him. He was Angelo.

"This is the gentleman?" Fortunata asked.

"He was there, talking to her," Angelo said in a tight, thin voice. "At Mother Perri's."

Singer sat quietly in his chair, looking at Angelo. I sat quietly too, looking at Fortunata. I wriggled a muscle in my neck, as an experiment, and found I had enough room to talk.

"Tell him to take his goddam knife away from my neck," I said to Fortunata.

Fortunata seemed not to hear me. "What did you have to say that Marcella Cipriano found interesting?" he said.

"Tell him to take the knife away," I said.

Fortunata stared at me. "This is no time for bravery," he said. "Angelo is upset. He was in love with Marcella Cipriano."

The knife trembled. I felt it tremble. I was good and sore now. I hate this kind of stuff. I hate that helpless feeling.

My feet were flat on the floor. The chair was the occasional type with narrow arms, delicately balanced. I pushed with my feet and the chair went over backwards. I rolled aside and got my legs free and crawled around to the opposite side from where Angelo stood with his knife. He was a little slow on the pickup, slow enough so that I had time to get to my knees before he jumped me. I had hoped he would jump me. He was good and upset. He didn't know what he was doing. I could see the knife going up in the air and I knew it would throw him out of balance. I caught him with my right hand just below his lower left ribs and gave him a push. He made a half-turn, twisted to regain his balance, tripped against the chair and went down, dropping the knife. I made a dive for it, but Fortunata's long, thin hand got there first and scooped it up. When I stood up he was sitting in the chair again, calmly balancing the knife on the palm of his hand, staring coldly at Angelo.

"That was clumsy, Angelo," he said. "You must learn to coordinate your feelings with your physical alertness. You must not attack people in anger. You have no control."

Angelo stood and smoldered, but he didn't talk back. His chest was heaving.

"I thought Angelo probably knocked off Marcella," I said.

Angelo took a step toward me and Fortunata held up his hand. Angelo stopped.

"That was an unkind thing to say," Fortunata said.

"It's an unkind thing to slap a knife against a guy's throat," I said. "The hell with Angelo."

"Angelo, leave the room," Fortunata said.

Angelo walked out without a word. Fortunata looked at me.

"You are very fast, young man," he said. "Angelo might have killed you."

"I believe it," I said. "What made him think I killed Marcella?"

Fortunata shrugged.

"He saw you talking to her at Mother Perri's. He knew she agreed to see you. He got to the apartment about three-fifteen and found her dead. Naturally, the first person he thought of was you."

"Oh, naturally," I said. "Does he also think I killed Constancia Cipriano?"

Fortunata looked at me for a while with his chrome-button eyes. "I think not," he said.

"How does it happen," I asked him, "that the police have not yet been informed of the murder of Constancia?"

"The police? You have seen the interest the police take in the death of Marcella Cipriano. Besides, bambino, Angelo had no alibi. It would have been ridiculous to call the police. The police are impetuous."

"Not the ones I saw," I said.

Fortunata looked away. My conversation wasn't sharp enough for him.

"Mr. Batts," he said, "why did you come to me?"

"I had hoped you could give me some information."

Fortunata's eyes slipped over him slowly. "You are taking it upon yourself to investigate this death?"

"I am."

If Fortunata was amused, he didn't show it. He just kept going over Singer with his eyes. Finally he said, "Who are you, Mr. Batts?"

Singer smiled a little and shrugged his thin shoulders. It made his neck stick out even farther from his stiff collar.

"I am an innkeeper in a small town not far from here."

"And also an amateur criminal investigator, perhaps?"

He sighed faintly. He had said it with just enough edge to make it sound ridiculous.

"Look," I told him, "if you're worrying about whether Singer Batts can figure this out or not, you can stop worrying right now."

The chrome-plated eyes fastened on me. He didn't say anything.

"Who is paying you for the time and trouble?" he asked Singer.

Singer looked puzzled. "Nobody is paying me."

Fortunata laughed softly, throwing back his thin, delicate head. "Come now, Mr. Batts. Surely you stand to gain something by solving Marcella Cipriano's murder."

"You call it murder," Singer said.

Fortunata hesitated. It was the first time.

"Naturally," he said then, softly. "Naturally she was murdered."

"I need information," Singer said. "If you don't give it to me, I will get it somewhere else. But I would rather have it from you." He smiled. "I would consider it more official."

Fortunata got up and walked across the room. He paused over there for a while, then turned and walked back slowly. "What information do you want?" he asked.

"Who was Antonio Perotta?" Singer asked.

"Perotta? I don't know."

"Constancia Cipriano married a man named Antonio Perotta. They lived here until the war. Antonio Perotta was killed at Anzio."

"You know more than I already," Fortunata said. "What do you expect of me?"

"I want to know what Antonio Perotta did while he lived in Chicago."

"But, Mr. Batts, I wouldn't know that."

"You could find out."

"Perhaps. But it would take quite a bit of time."

"We have a little time. Not much." Singer stood up. I stood up too. "You will see what you can find out about Antonio Perotta and let me know. You may get in touch with me through Professor Howard Jackson of the University of Chicago. He will take a message for me."

Fortunata stared at him. It was clear that he was not used to being spoken to in this way and he didn't know exactly what to make of it. While he was wondering, Singer shot in the next punch.

"One more thing I want to know," he said. "Where is Nick Andrews?"

"I beg your pardon?" Fortunata said.

"Nick Andrews, husband of Constancia Cipriano. Where is he now?"

"Mr. Batts—" There was a tone under his voice now, like the tone a sharp knife blade would make if drawn lightly across the E string of a violin.

"None of that, Mr. Fortunata," Singer said. He used his own sharp tone. It's pretty sharp. You never quite expect it. "We found the empty room and the paper carrying the legend of the Black Hand. A crude device, Mr. Fortunata, for this age. It lowers you in my estimation."

"Indeed," Fortunata said.

"Indeed," Singer said.

He walked across the room. On a small table near the window were a couple of old books. They had fancy bindings and were thick and heavy. I hadn't seen what was printed on them. The edges of the paper were faded and stained. Singer picked one of them up.

"The Advancement of Learning," he muttered, "London Stationers, 1622."

He riffled through the pages.

"You bought this?" he asked Fortunata.

"I dabble in old books," Fortunata said. "That one is a work by Francis Bacon, the great English—"

"Yes. You bought this?"

"Yes, I did."

"How much did you pay?"

"Twenty-eight thousand dollars," Fortunata said. "A bargain."

"You were duped," Singer said. "It is worth perhaps five dollars, as a reproduction of an edition which was a fraud in the beginning."

Fortunata's eyes gleamed but he didn't take them off Singer.

"Is that so?" he said.

"Yes. The work published in 1622 was in Latin," Singer said.

There was a pause. Fortunata kept staring at Singer.

"Who are you?" he asked finally, for the second time.

"You have my name and the telephone number of a friend of mine," Singer said.

"Yes," Fortunata said. "What was it you asked me a few minutes ago?"

"Where is Nick Andrews?" Singer said.

After a moment Fortunata reached up and pulled that cord again. Angelo came into the room. He glowered at me. He glowered pretty well.

"Bring in the Andrews boy," Fortunata said.

Angelo went out. A couple of minutes later he came back, with Nick. Nick looked dazed and sleepy. He recognized us and smiled, but he didn't say anything.

"We will require his assistance," Singer said.

"Why?" Fortunata said.

"We will require it," Singer said. "You will release him to us."

I braced myself. It seemed to me that Singer had pushed the thing one step too far. Fortunata was the man who gave orders, not the one who took them. I watched his eyes. Also I watched Angelo for signs of the knife. It was hard to watch both of them at the same time. Then Fortunata spoke.

"I will make a bargain with you," he said to Singer. "I have good reason to believe that Mr. Andrews murdered his wife in a fit of rage. She had left him."

"I will prove otherwise," Singer said.

"Very well. If you can prove otherwise, within thirty-six hours, I will release Nick Andrews. If not, we will deal with the situation in our own way."

"Thirty-six hours is a short time," Singer said.

"For a man of your brilliance," Fortunata said, "it should be sufficient time. That is my bargain."

"I require Nick Andrews' assistance," Singer said.

Fortunata looked at Angelo. I didn't see anything happen between them. I guess something did, because the next thing Fortunata said was, "All right, Mr. Batts. I will release Mr. Andrews to you now. You know us well enough to know that he can't escape. You will not try to hide him from us."

Singer's thin shoulders hunched up and back. "We will see what develops," he said. "Meanwhile, I also require the information about Antonio Perotta."

"Yes," Fortunata said. "Antonio Perotta."

Singer went to the door and Nick and I followed him.

"Just a moment."

We stopped. I turned around, but Singer didn't.

"If Caesar Fortunata gives you information," he said, "it has a price."

"Of course," Singer said quietly.

"Caesar Fortunata will be kept informed, by you, of the progress of your investigation."

"Naturally," Singer said.

"If you find the murderer of Marcella Cipriano, you will let me know at once."

"After notifying the police," Singer said definitely.

"No!" His voice was sharp as a knife. "Not after the police. *Before* the police."

"But it will be necessary for the police to take action."

Fortunata's face wrinkled up in that smile. I didn't like it. I didn't like it at all.

"I will take action," he said, "more intelligent action than the police." He paused and the smile got a little bigger. "I have more—facilities."

I didn't doubt it. I didn't doubt it for a minute, and when we got to the street it was clear enough that Fortunata's facilities had already been put to work. As the three of us got into my car and pulled away from the curb, another car pulled out behind us, half a block behind. It was a green sedan with whitewall tires and there were two men in it.

One of the men was Angelo.

CHAPTER VIII

It was one o'clock and we stopped at a restaurant on Chicago Avenue. I was tired from the long night before and I ate quite a lot. Singer ate practically nothing and Nick picked over a few items on his plate and stared into space. After a while, Singer got up and went to a phone booth. He came back almost at once.

"Caesar Fortunata has left a message with Professor Jackson," he said.

"Already?" I said.

"I expected him to be prompt," Singer said.

"What was the message?"

"He said that if we would be patient for a few minutes, Angelo would meet us here and give us the information."

"Angelo has been following us around in a green sedan. If he knew the information, why didn't he give it to us before?"

"I suppose there are systems of communication in a well-knit organization like Mr. Fortunata's."

"I suppose so."

I glanced up from my broiled salmon and looked into Angelo's face. He stood stiffly like a soldier at attention and his dark eyes felt of me the way a wrestler feels for a hold. I didn't like Angelo. I wondered whether Mr. Fortunata had given him back his knife.

"Sit down," Singer said pleasantly, but Angelo only shook his head.

"Antonio Perotta," he said in a flat, monotonous voice, like a schoolboy reciting a poem. "He married Constancia Cipriano in 1942. He worked as a bookkeeper for the Spark-EE Corporation on the West Side. He was an educated boy. He was drafted in the Army in 1943 and he got killed in the war in 1944."

"What is the Spark-EE Corporation?" Singer asked.

"I don't know," Angelo said.

"Do you know what department Antonio Perotta worked in?"

"No."

"Do you know anything else at all about him?"

"No."

"Did you know Constancia Cipriano?"

"No."

"Thank you," Singer said. "And please thank Mr. Fortunata for me. It was a pleasure to meet him."

Angelo turned and walked away, smooth and tight under his neat, wide shoulder pads.

"He's still sore at me," I said.

"Undoubtedly."

"It was only self-defense."

"It is insulting to a member of Angelo's circle to defend oneself against attack."

"He's easy to insult. If he pulls that knife again, I'll kill him."

"Please forbear," Singer said. "Angelo is more useful alive than dead. I think, in fact, he is not angry at you. I think he is angry at the murderer of Marcella, his sweetheart—as I would be. I think he plans to apprehend the culprit himself. At that point, I suggest you refrain from getting in his way."

Nick spoke up for the first time since I'd shooed him out of Marcella's apartment the night before.

"I remember now," he said. "Constancia told me her first husband was a bookkeeper."

"Did she mention the Spark-EE Corporation?" Singer asked.

"No. I never heard of that."

I went on with my dinner and Singer sat patiently and waited, chewing a stalk of celery and staring into space. After a while he said, "Excuse me for a moment."

He left the table and went to the telephone booth again. I saw him look through the directory, pick up the phone and dial and I saw him talking to someone. He hung up and dialed another number and I saw him talking again and finally he came back to the table.

"The Spark-EE Corporation," he said, "is a firm engaged in the manufacture and distribution of a patented beverage that tastes like carbonated grape juice. The chief accountant of the Spark-EE Corporation is a gentleman named Moynahan, who can probably tell us something more about Antonio Perotta. Mr. Moynahan will be in until five o'clock. We will call on him."

"All right," I said. "I'll skip the dessert."

Suddenly Nick started to talk. He talked as if it were a big effort for him to do it, but it had to be done.

"Look," he said, "you fellows have been nice to me, but you don't have to do all this. Why don't you just let me out and go about your business?"

There was a pause.

"Your business," Singer said quietly, "is currently everybody's business."

"But I don't want you to go to a lot of trouble—" I tumbled to what was really on his mind. It made me sore for a minute, but then I realized he had no way of knowing.

"I know what you're thinking," I said to him. "You're thinking we're a couple of hicks from nowhere who have got into something too deep for us. You think we're just mixing everything up. You think we don't know what to do.

"This is Singer Batts here," I said. "You may never have heard of him. He knows about these things. He's worked out things tougher than this one and he'll work this one out too. Just relax. Just do whatever he says and everything will work out all right. Believe me."

He didn't say anything. I don't know whether he took it all, hook, line and sinker, or whether he just quit arguing. But he kept quiet, which was the main thing I wanted.

Singer was embarrassed, but I passed over that.

The Spark-EE Corporation was housed in a low, flat, red-brick building on the far West Side. I parked the car and we went into the building. Moynahan's office was near the front. It had a frosted glass door, an outer office with an elderly lady at a small desk. Inside the private office there were some plywood paneling, a water fountain, a liquor cabinet, a big desk and a row of filing cabinets. The lady said Mr. Moynahan would be right in.

The chairs were leather, very old and comfortable. Singer and Nick and I sat down in them. The door opened and Mr. Moynahan came in.

CHAPTER IX

Mr. Moynahan was big and rangy, with heavy shoulders and big, freckled hands, an Irish grin and a shaggy crop of reddish-brown Irish hair. He had no brogue. But you would never have taken him for a foreigner to Erin. He was friendly and jovial in that special Hibernian way. He was a guy you liked.

Also he looked familiar to me. But I couldn't place him. He asked if we'd like a drink and I said yes. He went to the liquor cabinet, which opened into a portable bar, complete with a freezing unit and all, and I just sat there and watched him mix me a bourbon and soda that looked delicious while he made it and tasted even better when I got it in my mouth.

Moynahan had one too, but Nick and Singer declined. This was unusual for Singer. He always drinks some whisky when he's working on a crime. But not this time. I guessed he was thinking too hard.

Singer made the usual apologies about disturbing Mr. Moynahan during office hours and so on and so on and then he said, "You have read, I presume, about the murder of a dice girl named Marcella Cipriano."

Mr. Moynahan's eyebrows went way up.

"I read about her death," he said. "I didn't read about murder. The police seemed to think it was suicide."

"That is true," Singer said. "I happen to believe it was murder."

"Oh. Well," Moynahan said, "just who are you, if you don't mind?"

"My name is Singer Batts. My friend here is Joseph Spinder. And this is Nick Andrews. We came into the matter of Marcella Cipriano somewhat indirectly and by a set of circumstances that would take too long to describe. Along the way, we ran into the name of Antonia Perotta. We found that Perotta was formerly employed by the Spark-EE Corporation and I took the liberty of imposing upon you for some information about him."

"Antonio Perotta is dead," Moynahan said. "He was killed at Anzio. Too bad. He was a bright lad."

"Just what were his duties as a member of your accounting staff?"

"Antonio—let's see—he was in the Accounts Payable Department. He was a junior bookkeeper. He worked hard and tended to his own business. Everybody liked him. He married a girl who worked for me at the same time, a little Italian girl—wait a minute! Her name was Cipriano too! Her first name—I can't quite remember—"

"Constancia," Singer said.

"That's it! He married Constancia Cipriano a few months before he was drafted."

He looked at Singer with a puzzled twist between his eyes.

"Do you suppose Constancia Cipriano was related to this Marcella girl who committed suicide—or was murdered?"

"They were sisters," Singer said. "Constancia is also dead—of murder."

Moynahan was shocked. He had lifted his glass to his lips and when he heard this he stopped suddenly, holding the glass stiffly and peering at Singer over its top.

"No!" he said.

"Yes, I am sorry to say," Singer said. "The other day, here, in her sister's apartment."

"I can't believe it! She was murdered?"

"Quite completely," Singer said.

"But—why?"

"We don't know that," Singer said. "We hope to find out. The logical place to start is with her husband, Antonio Perotta. We have no indication of any motive for her murder.

"It is possible that the motive is old, though the crime is still quite young. However, the crime grows older by the minute and the less time we waste, the better. What can you tell me about Antonio Perotta?"

Moynahan mixed another drink for himself and one for me. He settled back in his chair, balancing the glass on his knee, and began to tell us about Antonio Perotta.

"He was a well-trained, ambitious kid," he said. "A college graduate with a good record. He came to me for a job at a time when I needed a good young fellow in that department. I hesitated because of the draft situation. We were trying to hire older men. But he said he had defective vision and wasn't likely to be inducted. This was true. He wore thick glasses and he couldn't see much of anything without them. So I hired him.

"As I say, he was a hard worker and he got things done. Everything was always neat and tidy, no loose ends. He rarely worked overtime, because he got everything done during office hours. He was an ideal employee."

"When was it he started work with you?" Singer asked.

"That would be hard to remember. Let me see—" Moynahan passed his big, freckled hand across his forehead. "It was after the inauguration of the draft, that would have been—it was before Pearl Harbor. It was in the spring of 1941. I can't tell you the day and month without looking up the record."

"How big a business does the Spark-EE Corporation do in a year?"

Moynahan looked at him.

"Well, that's a question I shouldn't answer."

"It may be quite important," Singer said. "Could you give me a rough idea of the class in which the Spark-EE Corporation stands, financially, as to gross sales; or how much credit could it command if necessary?"

"I might as well tell you," Moynahan said. "You could look it up in the papers. Our balance sheet is published regularly along with everybody else's. We do a gross business per annum of approximately two million dollars."

"That has been constant over a period of time?"

"For the past ten or fifteen years. The product had an almost immediate success and it was well-financed and managed right from the beginning. We're not a large corporation, but we return a reasonable profit to the stockholders and maintain a substantial reserve. It's what you'd call a comfortable business."

"I see. Could you tell me anything specific about Antonio Perotta's duties with your firm? Did he have any unusual job, anything out of the ordinary for a junior bookkeeper?"

"Yes, he did," Moynahan said. "I suppose every business has its own idiosyncrasy. Ours was the inventor of Spark-EE, a Mr. Charles Angora. He was the chemist who developed the formula and sold it to the present stockholders on a royalty basis. Mr. Angora was an eccentric."

"How eccentric?" Singer asked.

Moynahan laughed. The wrinkles around his eyes ganged up and his face shook a little.

"He was about as eccentric as a man can be. I had heard about inventors with strange quirks of personality, but I never saw anybody like this Angora."

"This has something to do with Antonio Perotta's work?"

"Yes. Angora, the inventor, accepted a royalty agreement with the Spark-EE firm based on five percent of the gross sales."

"Isn't that rather high?"

"Not in this business. It would be high in certain commodities where the cost of production is heavy and the unit of sale is big and therefore limited. But it doesn't cost much to produce Spark-EE and the gross profit is satisfactory. A five-per-cent royalty is fair enough. During the initial stages of development and distribution, of course, Angora didn't make much. But after the thing got rolling, his five percent brought him a comfortable living. His monthly payment for the past ten years has run between seven and ten thousand dollars."

"This is an eccentric?" I said.

Moynahan laughed again.

"Sometimes the crazy ones make the most of anybody," he said. "Angora was as nearly crazy as I would ever want to be. For one thing, he insisted that his royalties be paid in cash. He wanted no truck with checks, even certified checks. He wanted cold cash, coin of the realm, solid currency. Seven to ten thousand a month in cash is a lot of cash. I don't know whether he invested in other businesses, whether he spent it, or whether he played it all on the horses. But that's the way he took it. In cash."

"The monthly period of payment is unusual too, isn't it?" Singer asked.

"Somewhat. A royalty agreement usually provides for quarterly or semi-annual payments. But Angora asked for it every month and it didn't really make any difference to us. Of course, we were always a little behind. We didn't pay him the first of May for the April business. The cash he would get in March, say, would be for January business."

"How was the cash delivered to Angora?" Singer asked.

"That's where Antonio Perotta comes in," Moynahan said. "That was one of his jobs. Before we hired him, I delivered the royalty myself. I don't know why. I'm no more trustworthy than the next fellow. But of course I'm bonded and after I got to know Antonio well and saw I could trust him, I delegated the delivery job to him. We got him bonded for ten thousand dollars and from then on, he took care of the delivery. Antonio, as accounts payable bookkeeper, made out the royalty tab each month, which I okayed and sent to the bank for cash. Brinks delivered the cash to us and we packed it in a valise. Antonio carried a gun, of course."

"Brinks?" I said.

Moynahan laughed again.

"Antonio Perotta, I gather," Singer said, "would deliver the cash, get Angora's receipt and produce the receipt when he returned."

"That's right. He usually held the receipt overnight. Angora lives in a big old house on the North Side and Antonio had to go near it to get to his own home. It was easier for him to make the delivery after work in the evening and bring the receipt back in the morning."

"What does this guy, Angora, the inventor, look like?" I asked.

Moynahan turned his big head toward me.

"I don't know," he said. "I never saw him."

"I beg your pardon?" I said.

"That's true," Moynahan said. "That was another of his eccentricities. He lived alone in this big old house and he never went out, as far as I know. He was never in sight when we took him the money."

"I don't understand," I said. "How did you make the delivery? How did you get the receipt?"

"The front door was unlocked," Moynahan said. "We took the money inside, into a little study off the reception hall. There was a desk there. We piled the money up on the desk and picked up the receipt which had been signed in advance. We filled in the amount of the royalty ourselves."

"Isn't that a risky way to do business?" Singer asked.

"It was for Angora," Moynahan said. "It didn't matter to the firm. We had a tab for the cash, the amount of the royalty was subject to periodic audit and we had Angora's signature on a receipt."

There was a pause. Singer was deep in thought.

"Wouldn't that leave a big opening for the delivery boy?" he asked finally.

"How do you mean?"

"I mean—wouldn't it have been an easy matter for, say, Antonio Perotta to fill in a fictitious amount on the receipt, lower than the actual amount, and to pocket the difference?"

Moynahan laughed again, indulgently this time.

"But that would be too great a risk. No accountant would ever take it. The receipt was in duplicate. One came back to the office. That would have to be correct. It would have to jibe with the tab and with the monthly balance sheet. The duplicate might be altered, but sooner or later, Angora would be informed of what he should have received and the thing would come to light. We mailed him a balance sheet every month. I don't know whether he ever looked at them, but there was always the chance that he might. And when he did, it would be curtains for that delivery boy. No, I don't believe an intelligent man would take that chance, least of all a boy as bright as Antonio Perotta."

"That is reasonable," Singer said. "Nevertheless, I am convinced that somehow Antonio Perotta came by a large sum of money, that he came by it illegally or dishonestly and that it has something to do with the murder of Constancia Perotta and of Marcella Cipriano."

Moynahan looked serious. He studied Singer's face carefully, then he looked at me. He got up and mixed a couple of drinks.

"Do you realize what you're saying?" he said. "You are accusing a dead man of the crime of embezzlement. In our profession, there is no greater crime."

"I am aware of that," Singer said. "But I am not accusing Antonio Perotta of any crime. I am only trying to find out whether it would have been possible for him to commit it. Because if it had been possible for him, it would have been possible for someone else. It might, for example, have been possible for Constancia Cipriano."

Moynahan laughed again, loudly.

"Little Constancia? Ridiculous!" he said. "You don't know her. She was a cringing little violet if I ever saw one. Beautiful and delicate and timid and all the things a thief never is. Oh, I know there are exceptions. But I knew Constancia very well. I just can't see your reasoning."

"I may well be wrong," Singer said. "I have been wrong in my life. I hope I'm wrong now. But I know that Constancia had money, that her second husband had very little, and that after Constancia's death a large sum of money turned up in somebody else's hands in another state."

"A large sum of money?"

"Quite large. Two hundred thousand dollars or more."

Moynahan whistled. "How do you mean—it 'turned up in somebody else's hands'?"

"I can't go into it all now," Singer said. "I am glad to have had this chance to talk with you. Tell me one more thing. After Antonio Perotta left your firm, who took over delivery of the money to Mr. Angora?"

"Well, I did it myself for a while. Then I picked one of the old trusted employees, a man named Caspar Foley, to do it. Old Caspar is sound as a dollar."

"Would it be possible for us to talk to Mr. Angora, the inventor?" Singer asked.

"About that I wouldn't know," Moynahan said. "I can tell you where he lives, but whether or not he'll see you, I couldn't say."

"He has no household staff, no secretary?"

"Not that I know of. I think he has a cleaning woman who comes in and takes care of the old house. I never met her, nor anyone else there for that matter."

"I would appreciate your letting me have his address."

"Certainly. It's on Bellevue Place, west of the Boulevard, a brownstone house, two stories, one of those quiet streets that used to be so tony in the old days. It's pretty faded now and run down."

He gave us the number of the house. As we were leaving, he said, "Gentlemen, you've made me nervous. I'll probably lie awake all night, trying to figure out who's stealing from the company and how much."

"I trust we'll find an answer for you," Singer said. "Thank you again."

"Please keep in touch with me," Moynahan said. "I'm available at the office every day from nine to five."

"We will be in touch with you," Singer said. "By the way—you are insured against loss by embezzlement?"

"Naturally," Moynahan said.

"Would you mind telling me the name of the firm that writes this insurance for you?"

Moynahan hesitated, looking Singer over. Finally he shrugged and said, "I don't know why not. It's the Northwestern Casualty Company. Offices at Michigan and Wacker Drive."

"Thank you," Singer said.

"If you have any idea of talking to the insurance people," Moynahan said, "about what you've just told me, I'd appreciate it if you'd let me know first." He chuckled. "Those are things I'm supposed to know about."

"Of course, Mr. Moynahan," Singer said. "You've been very helpful and I appreciate it. Thank you."

We went out and got in the car again.

"Very well, Joseph," Singer said. "Drive to the scene of the crime."

I drove there. I had no difficulty finding the way. I'd been there before.

CHAPTER X

It was late afternoon now. Long shadows crept down into the canyons of the Loop and spread across the streets of the North Side. People on the streets moved along fast, getting home from work.

I stopped across the street from the apartment building on Delaware, where Marcella Cipriano had lived. We went up to the door and Singer rang the bell marked "Manager."

The lady was tough, well-dressed and carefully tended, like a garden that's been growing all summer and is just about to dry up for the winter.

Singer smiled pleasantly.

"I understood you might have a vacancy," he said.

"What makes you think so?" the manager asked.

"Rumors get around," Singer said. "I am a scholar. I am visiting the city for a while and I plan to do considerable work at the Newberry Library. This is my assistant and this gentleman is a friend. There will be two of us only, no children and no pets. This place would be convenient for me—provided I like the apartment and the rent is equitable."

"I don't know what you consider equitable," the manager said, "but the only apartment I have is one-fifty per month."

There was no getting around it. Singer Batts just didn't look like a hundred and fifty smackers a month. The lady couldn't see it anywhere on him.

"May we see it?" Singer asked.

She looked from him to me, at Nick and back to him. I knew how she felt. You can't always tell by the outside, and a vacancy is a vacancy in any neighborhood.

"It's not quite ready to show," she said. "I haven't had the bed made up."

"I'm sure we can overlook that," Singer said. "But if you wish, we can return later."

Later she probably had a date.

"No. If you really want to see it," she said, "I'll show it."

She reached up behind the door and got a key. We followed to the elevator. She pushed the button for the fifth floor.

We got out and followed her down the hall to the door of Marcella Cipriano's apartment. Singer looked at me behind her back and I nodded. Nick's face was tight and drawn. Inside it looked like any vacant apartment.

The air was fresh and they had certainly lost no time straightening it up. The torn furniture had been replaced. All the drawers had been put back where they belonged. There was no dust, no litter anywhere. There was so little of anything except glitter and freshness that I wondered what good it would do for Singer to look at it.

He went to the wide window on the outside wall of the living room and looked out. The Venetian blinds were up and there was a clear view of the building next door, twenty-five feet away across a driveway. He looked out there for quite a while. The drapes hung at the extreme edges and did not pull clear across the windows. The Venetian blinds were the only curtains.

He moved away from the window and went into the kitchen. He looked at the stove, the refrigerator, into the cupboards. He took down one of the plates and looked at the bottom of it.

"Very fine china," he remarked.

The manager leaned against the wall, waiting.

"We have only the best of everything," she said. "Naturally there's an agreement about breakage."

I wondered who was paying the damages on the shambles I had seen in there earlier that day.

"Of course," Singer mumbled.

We went through the living room into the bedroom, pausing to look into the bath. I had never seen such a clean bathroom in all my life. You could see yourself anywhere you looked.

The bedroom was just as neat as the rest of it. There was a spread on the bed, drawn up and tucked under the pillows, although the linen hadn't been added yet. There was absolutely no sign that a very dead girl had been stretched out on it at four o'clock that morning.

Singer went to the closet and opened the door. He stepped inside. I saw his eyes travel upward toward the hooks that stretched across one wall. I looked at the same place. I would never forget the position of the hook from which Marcella Cipriano had been hanging and in order to show Singer which one it was, I reached up and pulled on it gently with my fingers, as if testing its strength. Around the edge of the hole where the hook screwed into the wall was a faint line of fresh putty. It was the only sign so far that anything had had to be fixed up, and you wouldn't have noticed it if you hadn't been looking.

I stepped back out of the closet and the manager looked at me with suspicion.

"The hooks are good and strong," she said.

"They feel like it," I said. I wondered what she was thinking.

Singer came out of the closet and looked around the room. He had taken a lot of time and the manager was getting impatient. She kept looking at her wrist watch.

"I'm sorry to keep you," Singer said. "If you have an engagement, please don't wait for us. I am a man of some deliberation."

He smiled his warmest smile. It made him look young.

The manager said, "Well—please be sure the door is closed when you leave. I'll be in my apartment. You can stop in there."

"Of course," Singer said.

She went out.

"That was the hook, Joseph?" Singer asked.

"Yeah," I said.

"And this is the same bed?"

"I would say so."

He got up and leaned over and pulled the spread away from the pillows. He pulled the pillows off the bare mattress and studied it near the headboard. The mattress fitted very tightly against the headboard. He pulled it back as far as he could and peered down in between the mattress and the headboard. His long fingers went down in there and groped around. Finally they came up. He held something up to the light. It was a hair. It was hard to be sure, in the dim light, but the hair seemed to have a reddish cast.

"Marcella Cipriano was a blonde," he said.

"Well, but after all," I said.

"Angelo is not red-haired."

"No. But that might have been there a long time."

"Perhaps. But we'll save it."

He pulled an envelope out of his pocket and dropped the hair into it and put the envelope back in his pocket. He glanced around the room once more, turned off the light with the switch beside the door and we went back to the living room.

"Nick," Singer said, "show us how you discovered Constancia's body."

"She was lying there," Nick said, "on the floor by the telephone. I came in the door here—"

"We will go through the motions," Singer said. "Joe, you be the corpse."

I lay down on the floor beside the telephone table a few feet from the door. Nick showed me how she had been lying, with her legs drawn up toward her chin, one arm flung out behind, the other pillowing her head. Her eyes had been open.

Nick went out into the corridor. Singer closed the door. Singer stood by the door, looking first at me, then at the big window with the Venetian blinds that looked out across the driveway to the next building.

The door opened and Nick came in.

"Do exactly what you did when you discovered the body of your wife," Singer said.

Nick stopped just inside the door, looked around the room. He came over to me and went down on his knees.

"I didn't know what to do," Nick said. "I felt her heart and it wasn't beating. Her eyes looked funny, dead, sort of. I thought I ought to call somebody, but I didn't know who to call and I was afraid to call the police."

"What time was it?" Singer said.

"About two-thirty in the morning."

"What did you do then?" Singer asked.

Nick got up. He walked toward the telephone table, stopped, turned and walked across the room to the davenport and sat down with his back to the window.

"Try and remember," Singer said. "Was there a light on in the room when you came in?"

"The floor lamp here was on," Nick said.

"Do you remember whether the Venetian blinds were open, or whether they had been closed?"

"They were down," Nick said. "I don't remember whether they were closed or not."

"And you didn't happen to notice whether there was a light showing in the apartment across the driveway?"

"No."

"No maid or janitor looked in?"

"Yes!" Nick said suddenly. "Somebody looked in. She didn't come into the room."

"Who looked in?"

"Like you said—a maid or something. I was sitting on the davenport, facing the door, and it opened and a woman stuck her head in and looked around. She had a broom and a dustpan in one hand."

"Did she speak?"

"She just said, 'I'll come back later.'"

"And you didn't say anything?"

"Nothing. What could I say?"

"And what time did Marcella and Angelo return?"

"About three o'clock. They came in and they both looked at Constancia and at me and then Angelo said to Marcella, 'Here's a gun. Hold him here till I come back. Don't let him get away.' Marcella wanted to call the cops, but Angelo said no. He tore the telephone wires loose. He seemed awfully sore about something and I couldn't understand it. I hadn't said a word."

"Then," Singer said, "Angelo went out and Marcella told you to run away."

"That's right," Nick said. "I didn't know what I was running away from, but Marcella convinced me. I was scared and I'd been drinking and I was confused."

"And Marcella asked you to hit her in the head with the gun."

"Yes. She said that was so Angelo would think I'd gotten the gun away from her and run out of my own free will. She said that Angelo would beat her if she let me get away." Singer sat down at the telephone table and put his head in his hands. There was a long silence. Finally he looked up.

"I believe I understand the sequence," he said. "Now it is necessary to sort out the characters. One more question, Nick. When you left the apartment, did you see the maid anywhere, the woman who had looked in and said she'd be back later?"

"I didn't see any sign of her."

"Very good."

Singer got up. We all went out and downstairs and Singer knocked on the door of the manager's apartment.

"I'd like to give it some thought overnight," Singer said.

"I can't hold it without a deposit," the manager said.

"That's quite all right," Singer said. "I'll take that chance. One thing—you offer maid service, of course."

"Naturally."

"When is your maid service done? That is, what time of day usually?"

The manager stared at him.

"In the daytime," she said. "When did you think?"

"Even for people who work nights?"

"Certainly. There's always a chance to do it sometime during the day."

"But you have no maids who work at night."

"No. We'd have to pay overtime for night work. As long as we can get it done during the day—"

"Of course," Singer said. "Thank you."

We went outside and I started across the street to the car. Then I noticed Singer and Nick were no longer with me. I looked back and saw them walking toward the next building to the north. I caught up with them.

The foyer door of this building was open and we walked down the corridor to the back of the building, found a back stairs and climbed up to the fifth floor. Singer walked back halfway toward the front of the building and picked an apartment on our right. The plate on the door said, "Mr. & Mrs. Harvey White."

Mrs. White came to the door. She was a pale, stringy woman with a skirt too tight for her hips and a blouse too big for her shoulders. She kept picking at the front of it with the thumb and forefinger of her left hand. She looked at us with overgrown eyes.

"I wonder whether you could help us?" Singer said pleasantly, giving her his smile.

"I can't buy anything," she said quickly. "My husband went away without leaving me any money and he won't be home—"

"I'm not selling anything," Singer said. "I'm looking for information."

She was more frightened every second.

"About your next-door neighbors," Singer said.

"You're from a credit company?"

"Nothing like that, ma'am. Are you aware that a young lady was murdered in the apartment across the driveway—last night?"

"Murdered—!"

"Yes, ma'am. I am investigating that murder."

"Well, if you're a policeman—"

"I'm not a public policeman, ma'am."

"Oh. Well, I don't really know—how could I know—"

"I am a private investigator. A large sum of money is involved in this affair and I am engaged by an interested party. I thought perhaps you might have noticed something."

"Oh, no. I didn't notice anything."

"Well, would you mind if I came in for a moment? I'd like to look through your window."

She gave him a look.

"Through my window—?"

"Yes. I would like to know whether it is possible to see into the next-door apartment from your place here."

Her voice was unexpectedly bitter. "Oh, it's possible, all right."

Singer lifted his eyebrows. "Indeed?"

"My husband never had any difficulty."

"Your husband?"

"The lady next door wasn't very careful about pulling down her shades."

"I see. Well, ma'am," Singer said, "we men are—regrettably—human. Then it *is* possible to see into the next-door apartment."

"I'm sorry I said anything, but—yes, it is."

"But you never were interested in looking into the apartment yourself. Only your husband."

"Certainly. Why would I look into somebody else's apartment?"

"I am sure you wouldn't, ma'am. Could I impose on you to look into it myself from here? The young lady is dead. I'm sure she won't mind."

The fright came back when he used the word "dead." It scares most people.

"Well, if you must."

"I'm afraid I must. You don't have to admit me, of course."

"We can't stand here talking," the woman said. "Come in and have your look. Who murdered the girl?"

"We don't know, ma'am."

"Are the police working on it? Are they likely to come here?"

"Not likely," Singer said, stepping inside. "The police think it was suicide."

"Wasn't it suicide?"

She had lost some of the fright and was getting curious.

"No, ma'am."

He spoke with complete conviction. Nobody could doubt it.

"How do you know?"

"There were signs," Singer said.

He had gone to the window and was looking over at the next-door apartment across the driveway. Marcella Cipriano's place was only blank windows now, darkening with the evening. But it was clear that anybody sitting in the Whites' apartment could look directly into Marcella's apartment without craning his neck. And if the blonde beauty I had found hanging in the closet had been careless about drawing the curtains, I could see what the temptation must have been.

"You needn't answer this if it embarrasses you," Singer said, "but was your husband looking into the young lady's apartment at any time last night or early this morning?"

"My husband wasn't home last night. He was out of town on business. He won't be home until late tonight."

"I see."

Mrs. White was still interested in the murder-suicide angle.

"What makes you think she didn't commit suicide?" she asked.

"Well—it would bore you to hear all the details," Singer said. "There was the absence of contusions adjacent to the wound made by the rope; there was the position in which the body was found; there were signs of struggle in the bedroom; there were several things."

He paused and looked thoughtful and then said, "Evidence right now indicates the murderer was a woman, probably a jealous wife."

"A jealous wife?"

"Yes. Someone, perhaps, whose husband was carrying on a flirtation with the victim. The victim was very beautiful."

"Is that so?"

"Yes. I think I may safely say that suspicion definitely points to a jealous woman, a wronged wife."

"But murder—you'd have to be desperate to commit murder."

Singer gazed at her. Then he sat down on the edge of a chair and gradually let himself lean back in it, as if he were settling down for a chat. He put his hands together and looked at Mrs. White thoughtfully over his crossed fingers.

"Women are strange creatures, Mrs. White. Jealousy is frequently a long-repressed emotion which seethes below the surface but fails to break through until touched off by some small exasperation, often a very minor thing in itself. Such a thing, for instance, as what you told us about your husband peeping at the young lady next door. In fact, jealousy may exist where there is no more cause than that—a man finds another woman interesting to look at."

I watched the fright return to Mrs. White's face. I saw that Singer was watching it too.

"Please understand me," Singer said. "I am not suggesting by any means that you might have murdered that young lady next door—"

"I! I murder—that's ridiculous."

"Of course. You know it's ridiculous and I know it. But the ways of human beings are strange and the police have a way of ignoring the true character of their suspects."

"You said the police thought it was suicide."

"They do," Singer said. "I am trying to convince them otherwise."

"You wouldn't mention to the police—you wouldn't bring me into it?"

"Of course not, ma'am. I respect your privacy. But if the police should begin again to look into the case, I could hardly prevent their turning over every stone—"

"Wait. Wait! It wasn't a woman. It couldn't have been a woman. It was a man."

She spoke with conviction.

"You say that as if you knew it," Singer said.

"I do know. I saw them."

"Them? There was more than one man?"

"Yes. One came in early and then she came in and later—" Suddenly she stopped and her hand went to her mouth and she was staring at Singer.

"What am I saying?" she said.

"You are telling me," Singer said, "that you happened to look into the next-door apartment last night and saw two men."

She crossed the room. She dug into a bag of some kind on a chair and came back with her hands full of knitting. She worked at it very fast and hard, but it didn't look as if she was doing a good job.

"About what time was this?" Singer asked.

"I don't know," she said, speaking low. "I'm only telling you these things now so I won't have to talk to the police. You understand?"

"Certainly."

"It was very late—or very early this morning. I couldn't get to sleep. I got up and came in here and did some knitting and listened to the radio. I saw the light go on in the apartment and a man come in and then I didn't look any more for a while."

"And when you looked again?"

"It was a warm night and the windows were open. I could hear him moving around. Then I looked again. He was moving around the room over there, as if he was looking for something. He pulled drawers out and felt through them."

"Didn't it occur to you he might have been a thief?"

She looked frightened again. "I never thought—I should have called the police."

"Perhaps. Go on," Singer said.

"Well, he kept pulling out drawers and things and finally he started looking under the pillows on the davenport and on the chairs and he pulled them off and threw them on the floor."

"Very odd," Singer said. "What did he do then?"

"He looked around the living room for a long time, then he went into another room and I couldn't see him anymore."

"Could you tell what the man looked like?"

"Only that he was big and wore a black hat. I couldn't see his face very well. The Venetian blinds were down, but the slats were open—you know how they work. I could see that he was a big man."

"And what time did the young lady come in?"

"I'm not sure. I dozed off for a while and then I woke up again and the light was off in the living room but there was a light in the bedroom. Then the living room light went on again and pretty soon I saw the girl standing in the doorway and the man came across the room and the light went off. Then the bedroom light went off too."

"And you didn't hear anything? Any voices? Did the lady scream?"

"No, there wasn't a sound."

After a moment, Singer said, "About this second man."

"Well, that was an accident. I finally decided to go to bed and I went out to the kitchen and got a drink of water, and on my way back to the bedroom I saw that the light had gone on again and I saw this other man walk across the living room."

"You knew it was another man and not the same one you had seen before?"

"Yes. This was a small man in a black suit. I think it was a tuxedo."

"And did you watch this second man?"

"For a minute. He went through the living room and into the bedroom and a light went on back there. Then the light went off right away and he came back through the living room and turned off the main light and went out."

"The main light?"

"The bright overhead light. He left a lamp burning."

"Hadn't the lamp been on before?"

"No. He must have turned it on."

"Fouling up tactics," I said to myself out loud.

Mrs. White looked at me.

"I didn't mean you," I said.

"Who are you two anyway?" she said suddenly. "How do I know whom I'm talking to?"

"Well, ma'am," Singer said, "if it's important to you, this gentleman over here is Joseph Spinder. My name is Singer Batts. This other young man is Frank Smith. I would appreciate it if you would look at Mr. Smith and tell me whether you have ever seen him before."

She stared at Nick. After a while she shook her head.

"No," she said. "Should I have seen him?"

"Not unless you also happened to be looking into Marcella Cipriano's apartment three nights ago—Tuesday, that is."

"I wasn't," she said.

"Very well," Singer said. "We thank you. I will see you are not molested."

She didn't say anything more. She just stood and watched as we walked away along the carpeted hall to the elevator.

Outside we crossed the street and got in the car. As I pulled away I glanced in the rear view mirror. Sure enough, the green sedan pulled out too and followed us again and one of the two men in it was still Angelo.

CHAPTER XI

The house of Charles Angora, the inventor of Spark-EE, on Bellevue Place, was an old brownstone pile. It was dark. A flight of stone steps led up to the door and grass was growing up through them. A pane was broken in the glass window beside the door. The whole place looked haunted and unlived in.

Eccentric, I thought, is putting it mildly. Maybe Mr. Angora is a vampire.

The front door was unlocked. We went into the musty-smelling vestibule. There was a litter of papers and advertising matter on the floor. A name under the mailbox read "Charles Angora." The last three letters of the name were barely legible.

Beyond the vestibule was a narrow reception hall, and an open door on our left led to a small study, filled with old, worn leather furniture. A roll-top desk stood against the inner wall. The top was rolled back and there was a mass of papers of all kinds stuffed into pigeonholes and littering the desk top. A thick layer of dust covered everything in the room.

"Looks like Mr. Angora went away for a while," I said.

"A long while," Nick said.

We wandered into a dining room. It had a high ceiling and a big crystal chandelier. There was a massive oak table in the center of the room and a few chairs around the walls. The dust was just as thick in here as in the study. There were light switches on the walls, but when we pushed them, nothing happened. We made our way around by the light from the street lamp outside.

The kitchen was not what you would call modern. The range was an old gas model with a high oven and a hood over it. There was a long shelf and glass doors on the cupboards. There were dishes in the cupboards.

Singer opened a door in the kitchen wall. It opened on blackness. I almost stepped into it, then stopped myself in time. The moist odor of dirt floated up to us. There was a wooden stairway leading down.

I lit a match and found the first stair. I got my right hand on the railing and felt my way down into the darkness, step by step. Singer came behind me and Nick brought up the rear. Singer's breath felt good on my neck.

The floor of the cellar had been paved, but it was worn out now and there were pits in it. Some of the pits had water in them. We sloshed around, lighting matches. Singer took some of the matches and we got separated. I found myself in a coal bin. There wasn't much coal in it but there was plenty of dust. I had turned to come back out of it when I heard Singer call softly from nearby, behind the furnace. I felt my way over to his burning match. It went out just as I got there. I fumbled for another.

"There's a loose brick here," Singer said, tapping the cellar wall in front of us.

I pried at it with my fingernails and it came out. It came out too easily. It was meant to come out. I stuck my hand in the hole and it went into empty space. I groped around in there but couldn't feel anything but air.

Nick came over.

"Here," he said, holding out an iron bar. It was an old, rusted wrecking bar.

"Shall I pull the wall down?" I asked Singer.

"I think you'd better."

"What if old man Angora should happen to come home while we're tearing his house apart?"

"That would be unfortunate," Singer said.

I stuck the bar into the hole in the wall, got it hooked good and pulled on it. Three or four bricks came out, clattering dully on the floor. Singer stood beside me, lighting matches one after the other.

They all came out easily. I pulled bricks out by three's and four's. They fell in a pile at our feet and pretty soon I had a hole in the wall big enough to stick my head and shoulders through. Singer leaned forward with a match and peered into the hole. He reached inside and picked something out. He withdrew his hand. There was a skull in it. Human.

"My God!" Nick said softly.

I let him do the talking for both of us. I just swallowed.

Singer laid the skull on the floor and reached back into the hole again. He came out with a couple of arm bones, forearms. He put those on the floor too. He kept reaching into that grab bag, each time coming out with a couple more bones. By the time he had them all cleaned out, we had a complete skeleton on the floor, only it was all in a pile, not strung together and hooked up the way they are in museums and medical schools.

Then he reached in once more. This time he came out with a long envelope, faded and yellow. There was writing on the outside of it. I lit a match and held it so he could read it.

"To be opened in the event of my death," it said. "Antonio Perotta."

The ink had faded and turned yellow along with the paper and it was hard to read. But there was no mistake about the name of Antonio Perotta.

Singer had slipped the contents of the envelope out and opened a sheet of paper. I lit another match. He read it aloud to us.

I killed Charles Angora. I was delivering the royalty money from Spark-EE to him every month. One night he was in the study when I came with the money. He was an old man with a fragile head. I hit him just once and he died. I carried him down in the cellar. I found some loose bricks and made a hole in the wall and put him in there. I wrote this confession and put it in there too, later, in order to protect the innocent.

I kept on delivering the royalties to Angora, but I kept them for myself. I forged his name to the receipts. I hid the money—most of it. Some of it I gave to my wife, Constancia. She knew nothing about this. Only Marcella, my sister-in-law, knew about it. After I am drafted, the Spark-EE Corporation will continue to pay the royalty. I don't know who will deliver it. Marcella will make out the receipts and pick up the money. She will put it in our hiding place. Some of it she will send to my wife, Constancia.

I am in love with Marcella. We plan to wait till we have enough money and then go away somewhere. If I get back from the service, we will. If I don't get back from the service, it won't matter. Only Marcella knows where the money is. You'll have to ask her.

Antonio Perotta.

I looked at the pile of bones on the floor.

"So that's Charles Angora," I said.

Singer didn't seem to hear.

"The message on the envelope is scrawled in ink and fading away," he said. "But the message inside is typewritten and has not faded at all."

"Perotta didn't write it," Nick said.

"Not unless he came back to life just for that purpose and within the last few days," Singer said.

"Also," he said after a minute, "I would like to have somebody explain to me how an envelope that has lain in the dirt of a charnel house for many years can retain such a strong scent of perfume."

He held it up and I sniffed at it. It was strongly scented. Singer put it in his pocket. He leaned down with a match and studied the skull on the floor. It was a high, thin skull. All the teeth had fallen away except two, far back in the upper right jaw. I bent down to look. The two remaining teeth had large gold inlays that anchored them to the jaw. The gold was almost unrecognizable, but you could tell if you looked closely that it was gold.

Singer started upstairs. Nick and I went along. If there were going to be skeletons, I wanted to be where Mr. Batts was. I felt safer there.

Upstairs in the study, Singer started going through old papers and notebooks in the roll-top desk. In the upper left-hand drawer there was a pad of receipts, ordinary receipts for cash like you find in the stationery store. The name "Charles Angora" had been signed to half a dozen of them.

Singer pulled papers out of the pigeonholes in the desk. There were miscellaneous receipts from the gas company, the light company, some insurance receipts. There were no personal letters from anybody. None.

In one pigeonhole there was a snapshot. It was old and faded like the envelope we'd found in the cellar. It showed a skinny man in a bathing suit on the beach. His head was thrown back and he was laughing. His mouth was wide open. It was too faded to see whether he'd had any inlay work done, but you could see that the teeth were bad.

Singer turned the snapshot over. On the back was written: "Charlie Angora. 1938."

"He must have had at least one friend," I said.

"Somebody certainly took the picture," Singer said.

He put the snapshot in his pocket along with the confession. He looked around the study for a while, then he shook his head slowly a few times and walked outside.

As we pulled away from the curb the green sedan came along with us. They weren't making any attempt to be sneaky about it. They just kept in sight, taking it easy. I wondered how hard it would be to get away from them in case we wanted to hide Nick somewhere.

It would be impossible, I thought.

At Big Red's hotel we went up to Nick's room. I was groggy from lack of sleep. It was only nine o'clock in the evening, but it seemed later. I lay down on the bed. Nick sat in a straight chair.

Singer picked up the telephone and dialed a number.

"Mr. Moynahan?" I heard him say. "I regret having to disturb you at this hour. I regret even more to have to inform you that for a number of years now your firm has been paying royalties to a man who does not exist. I refer to Charles Angora."

He listened for a while.

"I have a conception of what it must mean to you," he said. "I have no time to explain now. I suggest that you examine your books carefully. You may find some clue that has passed unnoticed... I beg your pardon?... How long ago did he die? That is something we don't know yet. Good night, sir."

He hung up. A moment later he was dialing again.

"Dr. Sandefur?" he said. "There is a skeleton in the basement of a house on Bellevue Place. I must know how long ago the man died... A male skeleton, yes... Oh, I beg your pardon, this is Singer Batts... Yes, Doctor. I will meet you there at midnight." He gave the doctor the address of the Angora house. "Thank you, Doctor," he said and hung up.

I got my eyes open and watched him for a couple of minutes. He looked unhappy. His long face was drawn and paler than usual. He was looking at Nick.

"You loved your wife very much, Nick?" he said.

"I guess I did," Nick said. "I guess I didn't think much about it when I had a chance, when she was alive."

"I am very sorry," Singer said. "I am convinced that your wife—and her sister—were trapped by circumstances of which they had only the barest knowledge and even that was unwelcome, something they would have wished not to know, if they had had a choice. I am convinced that their deaths were unnecessary and that they died in the most tragic of all circumstances and with the most tragic of results: which is to say, they died in a trap in whose setting neither had had any part; and they died unnecessarily and without profit to the murderer."

There was a pause.

"Do you know who the murderer was?" Nick asked.

"No," Singer said. "I am confident he will be brought to light. But at the moment, I couldn't say his name."

I heard Nick get up from the chair and pace around the room. Finally he said, "If Constancia was in a trap, I think she must have realized it. I remember how something always seemed to be on her mind, something that frightened her. She'd never talk to me about it. I tried to get her to talk about it. But she didn't seem to trust me. That was one reason we had these fights. I kept thinking, 'If she doesn't trust me, what good is it?' I wanted to help her, but she wouldn't let me."

"I do not mean to be harsh," Singer said, "but I doubt that you could have helped her. She was caught in a way that would have rendered you as helpless as she."

There was a knock on the door. Singer spoke. The door opened. Big Red came in. I opened my eyes again.

"You got an answer to that ad," he said.

He handed Singer a slip of paper. Singer read it aloud:

"Mrs. Burton. Apartment 701. Telephone SUperior 7068."

The address was on Delaware. It was the same address Marcella Cipriano had, when she had one.

I heard Singer dialing a number again.

"Mr. Moynahan," he said after a moment, "does the name 'Mrs. Burton' mean anything to you? It does not? I see. Thank you."

He hung up.

"Do you know a Mrs. Burton, Nick?"

"No," Nick said.

"Did your wife, Constancia, ever mention a Mrs. Burton?"

"Not that I remember."

There was some more silence, and in the middle of it I felt myself going to sleep. I fought against it, but I didn't fight hard enough. The next thing I knew I was dreaming. I dreamed I was walking along a country road and I saw Marcella Cipriano walking toward me under the trees. It was a pleasant feeling and I ambled along, waiting for her to catch up with me. But when she got there, Marcella Cipriano had faded away and turned into Caesar Fortunata and he had a knife. I started to run. I ran and ran, without getting anywhere, and then I woke up.

CHAPTER XII

The room was dark. I looked over at the other bed, but nobody was in it. The light was out and Singer and Nick were gone. It was eleven o'clock.

Singer's like that. Considerate. Even if he needed me, he wouldn't wake me out of a sound sleep. And he wouldn't wait for me to wake up if he had his nose on a strong scent.

So now he was wandering around somewhere by himself and God knew where. So Nick was with him—but what the hell.

I wanted to go back to sleep. But I thought about the people we were up against in this thing and the nature of the case. I struggled up from the bed, washed my face, straightened my tie and put on my coat and hat. Then I went down and pounded on Big Red's door.

"Yeah," he said. "They went out through the lobby. Singer didn't say where he was going."

"Did they call a cab?"

"I don't know," Big Red said.

"Then how would they get anywhere?"

"Maybe they called a cab, I don't know."

"They didn't say anything at all to you?"

"They just said good night. What else would they say? But Singer shouldn't be out wandering around like that, Joe."

"That's what I am thinking. Listen, I'm going to look for him. First, I'm going to see Mrs. Burton. Then I'm going to this address on Bellevue. He's got a date there at midnight." I gave him the number of the Angora house. "If you don't hear from me in half an hour, call the cops and tell them where I've gone."

"I'll go with you."

"Then who will call the cops?"

"Look, Joe, about the cops, it don't really matter."

"All right. Let's go."

We went out to the car.

"Who takes care of the hotel when you're gone?" I asked him.

"It takes care of itself. It's a good little hotel."

"No hotel is that good."

"Look, Joe, if you don't want me to go along—"

"Don't be silly," I said. "With you I feel safe."

"I don't know. I haven't been in a tussle for quite a while. I try to stay out of them."

"I hope we'll stay out of it tonight."

I drove over to Delaware and parked across the street from the scene of the crime against Marcella Cipriano.

"These fancy places," Big Red said. "They're all locked up at night."

"I'll think of something," I said.

In the foyer we looked at all the names. There was no Mrs. Burton. The name under Apartment 701, the number she had given Big Red, was Samuel Dickinson. I rang that bell. I rang it two or three times, giving it plenty of ring. But no answer came through the speaking tube and no buzzer sounded to unlock the foyer door.

Big Red was wandering up and down in front of the mailboxes, looking at the names. I figured he was looking for unusual ones that he could put down in his encyclopedia. But all of a sudden he said softly, "Irma Steele. I know her. I know Irma pretty well. I don't think Irma would mind opening the door."

He pushed the button under Irma Steele's name. He pushed it again.

"You don't care who you get out of bed," I said.

"Irma is in and out of bed so much, she don't know the difference," he said.

"What if she has company?"

"Oh, I wouldn't disturb her that way. I just want her to open the door."

A sleepy voice came through the speaking tube. Big Red announced himself. The voice got high and shrill and profane. Big Red glanced at me and grinned. After a while the voice cooled off and Big Red said, "I just want you should open the door down here. Me and a friend—we've got to get in...

"The friend?"

Big Red said. "A guy I know."

The buzzer rang and I opened the foyer door. Big Red said good night to Irma and joined me.

"Quite a girl," he said. "She's from New York. Used to be a stripper. They called her 'Irma the Squirmah.'"

"Good for her," I said. "We're headed for Apartment 701. A woman who gave her name as Mrs. Burton. The name on the box said Samuel Dickinson."

"What if we run into Sam instead of Mrs. Burton?"

"Then we'll just have to apologize."

"Let us take the elevator, Joe. Seven flights is a long way. My wind isn't so hot any more."

We got in the elevator and rode up to the seventh floor. The halls were dim and quiet. No light showed under any of the doors. Number 701 was at the front of the building on our left as we approached. I knocked and got no answer.

"This is getting monotonous," I said. "Nobody's ever home here. Or else they're dead and can't come."

Big Red had his ear to the door.

"Somebody's home," he said. "And they're not dead. But they're not coming to the door either."

I listened against the door. Faintly from far off I heard a woman's voice. It wasn't a happy one. Big Red was fumbling in his pocket. He pulled out a thin steel instrument that was new to me and looked up and down the corridor. Then he inserted the thing in the lock and began to work on it.

"Freddie the Shark taught me this," he whispered. "Greatest second-story man in the business. They got him, though. Broke into a lady's apartment and she happened to have a gun and the sense to use it. Poor Freddie. Used to be a locksmith. Learned his trade."

He worked silently and expertly. The lock tumbled back with a light click and I closed my hand over the knob and twisted it quietly. The door opened. We walked into a dark living room.

It was the same kind of apartment Marcella had lived in, except that the layout was reversed, and there was no back service entrance. The bedroom was to our left from the front door, past the bath. The door between the living room and the little hall that led to the bedroom was closed, but there was a dim light showing below it. We heard the woman's voice again and then a man's, husky and whispering.

Big Red followed me to the door and I twisted that knob silently, opened the door and stepped through onto the thick rug of the hallway.

The woman was over against the far wall, cringing back against the window drapes. The light that we had seen came from the closet in the corner. It was enough. She was wearing a frilly negligee and little else, but most of the frills were hanging in ribbons, and there were slashes in the negligee, which had fallen from her shoulders, leaving her practically naked from the waist up. Her mouth was moving in an agony of fear, but the only sounds that came out were little moans and whimpers, like those of a puppy.

The man was facing her, his back to us. He had a knife. He was holding it now with the point just under her left breast, scratching at her flesh. The woman had backed away as far as she could and she looked as if she would push the wall out behind her if the man with the knife didn't lay off.

"Tell me now," the man said hoarsely. "Tell me where they went."

The woman shook her head back and forth desperately. It meant she didn't know. The knife flipped sideways, made another long slash in the negligee. It fell apart across her left thigh.

"Angelo," I said, trying not to shout it.

At the same moment I grabbed Big Red's arm and we hit the deck hard. I heard the swish of the knife and the thud as it went into the woodwork beside the door over us. Then Angelo was coming and I rolled and started up. By the time I got to my feet, Big Red had Angelo's coat all twisted up around his ears and Angelo wasn't moving.

The woman had fainted. She had just crumpled down to the floor and lay there in a ragged little heap. I picked her up—she was light as a feather—and stretched her out on the bed, covering her with the torn negligee as well as I could. I didn't try to bring her around. Let her get a little rest, I thought.

Big Red relaxed his grip on Angelo, who straightened his coat and stood like a statue, his eyes smoldering, the rest of him quiet and calm and poised. I walked over and pulled the knife out of the wall. It was a good knife. It balanced nicely in my hand. I looked at Angelo.

"What's the story?" I said.

Angelo shrugged.

"This is my girlfriend," Angelo said. "She stepped out on me. I was only trying to scare her."

"She's your girlfriend, my fanny," I said. "Marcella Cipriano was your girlfriend. Or do you own this whole house?"

Hatred dribbled out of his eyes when I mentioned Marcella Cipriano. Hatred—or pain. I didn't know. I had nothing against the guy, except that he kept pulling out that knife.

"All right," he said. "Your skinny friend came here."

"What happened to him?"

"I don't know. I was trying to find out. I never saw him leave."

"What the hell do you care whether he left or not?"

"I just do what I'm told," Angelo said. "I'm told to follow you two hicks. I do it."

"Hicks?"

The woman stirred on the bed. Big Red glanced at her. A strip of the negligee had slipped off one of her breasts. Big Red leaned down and replaced it carefully, without touching her.

"Was the Andrews kid with him?"

"He came in with him."

"How long ago did they come here?" I asked.

"An hour. Maybe more."

"How long did you wait?"

"Half an hour. Three-quarters."

"Then you came in and pulled the knife on the dame."

"She's a wrong twist. She's Sam Dickinson's girlfriend. She steps out on him all the time."

"Sam lives here?"

"No. He's got a good place. He keeps her here."

"Who is Sam Dickinson?"

"He's in the rackets."

"What rackets?"

"Big time. Con."

"Where did she get the name 'Mrs. Burton'?"

"That's a name Sam made up."

"All right—after Andrews and my skinny 'hick' friend came in here, who else came in?"

"Nobody. But there was somebody here waiting."

"Who?"

"I don't know."

"How do you know somebody was here?"

"Cigar butts in the ashtray. Your friend don't smoke."

"You're quite a detective."

He just looked over my head.

"If I give you this knife back, can I trust you not to use it on me?"

"No," he said. "You figure your own risk."

I balanced the knife for a little while, laid it flat in my palm and tossed it to him. He caught it by the handle and tucked it away somewhere inside his coat.

I went over to the bed and leaned over the girl. She was coming around and I stroked her forehead and waited until she opened her eyes.

"Mrs. Burton," I said, "I'm looking for Singer Batts."

She closed her eyes and turned her head away. I put my hand under her chin and pulled her head back.

"Look," I said, "I've got no knife. I don't want to hurt you. But I'm not kidding. My friend came up here and nobody saw him leave. I want to know where he went."

"I don't know," she said. She was pretty tired.

"All right. Did he go alone?"

"Yes."

"The hell he did."

"He went alone."

"Who was here with you when he came?"

She tried to turn away again but I held her by the chin. She wasn't a young kid, but she was good-looking and well cared for.

"If it's Sam you're worried about," I said, "you can quit worrying. I don't know Sam and I promise you Angelo won't say a word. If there was a guy here when Singer Batts came, all I want to know is who he was and where he might have gone. I give you ten seconds to tell me. After that, I turn you over to Angelo again."

I tried to make it sound reasonable and simple. But I meant it. If she didn't crack through with the information, I would let Angelo carve her into small bits. Angelo was the boy who could do it.

I guess I had the conviction in my voice. Anyway, she waited two or three seconds, staring at me and then she said, in a whisper I had to lean down to catch:

"Pat McCreery."

"Who's he?"

"A private eye."

"What would he want with Singer Batts?"

"He wants Nick Andrews."

Something clicked like a shutter in my mind.

"What does he look like?"

She didn't answer. I said it for her.

"Medium height, solid, got a scar on his chin. Looks like a bull. Sometimes goes by the name of Arch Whitney?"

"All right," she said.

"Where would he take Singer Batts?"

"I don't know."

"Where's his office?"

"In the Loop. Oak Street."

I looked at Big Red. He nodded, meaning he knew McCreery. I looked at Angelo, who shook his head, meaning McCreery wouldn't take Singer to his office. I looked back at the girl on the bed.

"Did you know Charles Angora?"

Her eyelashes flickered. The hesitation was a couple of seconds too long.

"No," she said.

"You're lying," I said.

"I'm not. I don't know anybody named Angora."

"Nuts!" Angelo said. "You know every other kind of cat in town. You must know an Angora."

She started up, blazing. The negligee fell into pieces around her. She lay back again, trying to gather it together.

"Put something on and come in the other room," I said.

She just lay there. I reached down and her right hand snaked up under her pillow and she came out with this gun. I stepped in close to the bed, grabbed her wrist and twisted. The gun dropped on the floor and Big Red picked it up.

"All right," I said, "come as you are."

I pulled her off the bed and she came along then into the living room.

"Call up your boyfriend," I said.

"Sam?" she shrieked.

"Not Sam. Pat. Pat McCreery."

"You're crazy."

"You know his number?"

"No."

"Then we'll look it up."

There was a drawer in the telephone stand. I opened it and found a black address book. I riffled through the indexed pages. On the M page was the name "Pat." The telephone number was DRexel 4892.

"Try this one," I said, pointing to the number.

"If I call him now," she said, "he'll kill me."

"If you don't call him now I'll kill you," I said, "or Angelo will."

She looked at Angelo. Angelo slipped his hand inside his coat. She sat down at the table, picked up the phone and dialed the number. It rang a long time and after a while I heard a man's voice answer.

She told him who it was.

"Ask him where Singer Batts is," I said.

"Where is Singer Batts?" she said.

The voice at the other end got loud and angry. She let it talk itself out. After a minute she said, "No… All right."

She started to hang up. I caught her arm and yelled into the phone, "Wait, honey!"

I listened at the receiver and pretty soon the man's voice said, "Mrs. Burton? Mrs. Burton, are you there?"

I nudged her.

"Yes, I'm here," she said.

There was some more talk at the other end and I got fed up. I nodded to Angelo. He came out with the knife, fast. He laid the knife against one of her breasts. Then he spoke to her, low enough to be convincing, loud enough to be heard, "First I cut off the nipples, one at a time. Then I go to work on the—"

"Wait!" yelled the voice on the other end. "What's going on there?"

Angelo had sounded like he meant what he said. I think he did.

The girl was scared now.

"Answer the question, honey," she said. "Just answer the question. Where is Singer Batts?"

There was a slight pause. Angelo jabbed her with the sharp point of the knife. It bled a little. She screamed.

"All right, all right!" McCreery said on the other end. "Singer Batts is right here in my apartment. If that tough friend of his is there, tell him he'll have to fight his way in."

"No, I won't," I told him. "I'm leaving Angelo here with your doll."

"No!" she yelled.

I hung up the phone.

"Don't leave that guy here with me alone," she said. "He'll kill me."

"No, he won't," I said. "Not if we don't have any trouble with Mc-Creery." I turned to Angelo. "Don't hurt the lady. Call McCreery's place in fifteen minutes. If I don't answer, get her on that phone again."

I started out with Big Red, then turned back and looked at her.

"Pretty fancy quarters for a chambermaid," I said.

"What are you talking about?"

"Of course you get time-and-a-half for doing the maid service at night. Maybe you can afford it."

"You're crazy," she said. "I'm not a maid."

"You were a maid at least twice. Once when Constancia Cipriano was strangled and once when her sister Marcella hung herself from a hook in her bedroom closet."

She just stared at me.

"Behave yourself, lady," I said. "Marcella was Angelo's sweetheart. He doesn't like the people who killed her."

Angelo was watching me, the knife quiet, poised in his hand.

"Where's your car?" I asked him.

"In back," he said, "with the driver."

"We'll go that way," I said to Big Red.

We went down the back stairs, around the building and through an areaway into the alley behind. The green sedan was parked a few feet away against a high board fence. A guy had just climbed out of it. He was leaning against the car door, massaging the back of his head, now and then shaking it. When we walked up he jumped and reached for a gun. Then he saw me and relaxed.

"What happened?" I said.

"Bastards slugged me," he said thickly. He was a squat, swarthy man with a badly pock-marked face. His clothes were too tight for him all over. His shirt collar stuck straight out in front.

"Who were they?" I asked.

"How the hell would I know?"

"They sneaked up behind you?"

"They didn't come from the front, for crissake!"

"All right. You didn't see anything and you don't know anything. Big Red and I are driving over to McCreery's place on Oak Street. If you want to tag along, all right. Only you better wait for Angelo."

He just climbed back into the sedan.

Big Red and I went back to Delaware.

"That little Angelo is a mean bastard," Big Red said.

"Mean and stubborn," I said. "He figures to get the guy who murdered his sweetheart. He figures to get him before Singer Batts does."

"He won't. He's dumb."

"Sometimes the dumb ones win."

"Not like him. They don't know how to act. You have to know how to act or you never get the right answers."

"He wouldn't care if he got the wrong one, just so he had somebody to carve up."

"That's right," he said.

"Well?" I said.

"So I better stay here and see that he don't carve up this Mrs. Burton prematurely."

"I hoped you'd say that," I said.

He went back to the apartment. I thought about how much sleep Irma the Squirmah was losing, getting up to let him in.

CHAPTER XIII

I drove fast over to McCreery's place on Oak Street. I walked up to his apartment on the second floor. I remembered the way all right. He opened the door right away, as if he'd been standing there waiting. He had a gun in his hand.

"Stop it," I said. "Angelo is sitting up with your pretty. He'd rather use that knife on her than anything. Where's Singer Batts?"

He didn't answer right away.

"I told Angelo to give me a ring in fifteen minutes," I said. "If I don't answer, Mrs. Burton will turn into ribbons. Twelve of those fifteen minutes are gone."

He stepped back from the door and I went in.

"Where is he?"

"In the bedroom in the back."

"*How* is he?"

"He'll be all right."

"He'd better be all right now."

"Go see for yourself."

I started to the bedroom. Through the open door I saw Singer stretched out on the bed. He was a mess. His face looked like a blob of bulk sausage. Both his eyes were swollen shut and there was a ragged cut along his left cheek. He was breathing normally all right, but he wasn't aware of it.

My stomach turned over a couple of times. The telephone rang. It rang again.

"Answer it," McCreery said.

"I'm not sure yet. It depends on how he is." I pointed to Singer.

"He's all right," McCreery said. "For God's sake, answer the phone."

It had rung three or four times now. It wouldn't ring much longer. Angelo wasn't very patient.

"Give me the gun," I said, passing him to get to the phone.

He handed it over.

I picked up the phone with my other hand and said, "Hello, Angelo?"

"When do I start cutting?" he said.

"Don't start. It's all right now. Come over here and meet us. Bring Big Red."

I hung up. McCreery was watching me. I kept the gun and went into the bedroom. I leaned over Singer and spoke to him. He didn't move. I shook him a little. He still didn't move.

"Here," McCreery said, holding out a little gauze package with a glass tube in it. "Smelling salts."

I broke the tube and held it under Singer's nose. Little by little he woke up. I waited, watching McCreery, holding the gun on him, wanting to pull the trigger, but unable to do it. McCreery's face was dead.

"What's the game?" I asked him. "What were you trying to get out of him?"

"Just the suitcase," he said.

"He doesn't have your lousy suitcase."

"It's in his hotel."

"No. It's in the bank."

"In the bank! You really put it in the bank?"

"It looked like the logical place for all that money. Whose is it?"

"Mine."

"Well, it's in a safe place."

"I can't get it out of the bank without a release."

"That's tough."

He didn't say anything.

"If you have a legitimate claim," I said, "all you have to do is present it."

"Aw, shut up," he said.

"Shut up, nuts!" I said. "You think you can push around a guy like Singer Batts, you're crazy. I've been looking all over for him."

"What else are you looking for?"

"A pot of gold, like you."

A new voice entered the conversation. An old, familiar voice and it sounded like music, even if it was a little cracked and very weak.

"Joseph," it said.

"Yeah," I said. "It's me, Singer. What did they do to you?"

"...not important," he said. "We must get to work."

"We must get you to bed," I said. "Can you get up?"

"Of course."

Little by little, stiffly, he sat up on the bed. He swung his legs over the side and groped for a foothold. Finally he stood up. He didn't look at Mc-Creery.

I gave him my arm and he made use of it. We walked around the bed, going slow. We got within eight feet of the door when a brand-new voice spoke up.

"Drop the gun." It was an unpleasant voice with a thick German accent.

He was behind me. I guess he must have stepped out of the closet. I dropped the gun. I watched McCreery scoop it up from the floor. Singer and I stood still.

"Well, well," I managed to say. "Good old Max."

"Yeah," McCreery said. "Get back on the bed."

Singer sighed.

"You don't seem to realize—" he began.

McCreery whipped the gun down and across Singer's face, where it was cut. Singer stayed on his feet, but I didn't see how.

I slugged McCreery in the face. His nose started bleeding. He lifted the pistol and I stepped under it and let him have it in the belly, one, two, three, four. I knew Max was behind me with a gun but I didn't care. I was sore.

Max shot me in the leg. It made a hell of a racket and it knocked me down. It was like being hit with a red-hot two-by-four. I fell into McCreery and he slammed me on the top of the head. Before I passed out I heard him say, "Let's get out of here."

* * * *

I came around slowly, painfully. Somebody was doing something to my leg and it hurt. I opened my eyes.

Big Red was leaning over the bed, doctoring my leg. He'd cut my pants away from it and was putting a bandage on me. He glanced up and grinned.

"Went right through," he said. "Clean as a whistle. I already poured the disinfectant in it."

"Yeah," I said.

I twisted my head. Angelo was standing over against the wall, watching Big Red. In the other room there was the sound of a typewriter.

"What the hell is that noise?" I asked the two of them.

"Singer found it," Big Red said. "He wanted to find out what the type looked like."

"I need another pair of pants," I said.

"We'll take a look," Big Red said. "McCreery was about your size."

"All his probably have blood on them," I said.

Big Red was going through a closet. He found a pair of gray flannel slacks. They were all right around the waist, but they were a little long. I turned them up at the cuffs. My leg was stiff but it didn't hurt much now. I limped into the living room. Singer was leaning over a portable typewriter, pecking something out on pieces of white paper, copying from the confession note we'd found in the Angora house.

He took the paper out of the typewriter and held it up alongside the other one. He looked at it for a long time. Then he said calmly, "I would say the two things were written with the same machine."

"McCreery," I said.

Angelo wandered into the room. He hadn't heard us.

"How's Mrs. Burton?" I asked.

He shrugged. "I don't know. She passed out before I left."

"Did you use that knife on her?"

"Nah. I just scared her with it."

"You must have scared her good and hard."

"I told you—she's a wrong dame. She's been two-timing Sam Dickinson for years and he don't believe it. Hell—only three weeks ago she went on a trip with another guy, clear to Washington, D. C."

I stared at him.

"Where was that again?"

He looked up.

"Washington, D. C. Why?"

"I just wondered. Who did she go with?"

"McCreery, the bull, I think."

I repeated it slowly to myself but out loud.

"With McCreery—to Washington, D. C."

"So what about it?" Angelo said.

"Nothing. It's a strange coincidence. Why would they go to Washington, instead of New York, or Bermuda, or Florida?"

"I wouldn't know," Angelo said. "McCreery was on some job. You find out those things. You know they're on a job, but you don't always find out what the job is."

"How do you find out?"

"You hear people talking."

Singer looked at Angelo. "When did they get back?" he asked.

"Who?" Angelo said.

"McCreery and the Burton woman."

"I don't know. They didn't come back together. The dame came back alone. It wasn't long ago. I heard somebody talking about how Sam Dickinson had been worried when he couldn't get her on the phone. That was three, four days ago."

"Very good," Singer said. "Remember that, Joe."

Singer observed Angelo for a while.

"Would you know," he asked, "whether McCreery was in town last night before Marcella Cipriano was murdered?"

Angelo's face tightened. His hand went inside his coat and his face turned a color I had never seen before. His eyelids drooped till they half-covered his eyes and his mouth twisted up on one side, down on the other.

"McCreery did it?" he said between his teeth.

"Not that I know of. We're just trying to get everybody into position."

"You get McCreery into position and I'll do the rest," he said.

"Take it easy," I said. "We don't know whether McCreery did it or not. We just want to know where he was. I know he was here after the murder. I don't know whether he was here before."

Angelo was halfway to the door, moving with his tight, catlike stride.

"I'll find out," he said.

I had a hunch he would.

"What happened to Nick?" I asked Singer.

"I don't know," he said.

"What did McCreery want from you?"

"I don't know that either. It was a baffling occurrence. And unpleasant."

I looked at his swollen, cut face and guessed at how unpleasant it must have been.

"How is your leg?" he asked.

"I can walk," I said. "What will we do about Nick?"

"We will have to catch up with McCreery first. Then we will see about Nick."

Big Red came into the room. He had a small envelope in his hand. He handed it to Singer.

"Found this in the Burton woman's apartment," he said. "Thought you ought to see it."

The envelope had the name of one of the airlines on it. Inside were two reservations to Mexico City. They were dated for the next day at five-thirty p.m. Singer looked at them. After a while he got up from where he was sitting. He took the two reservations and laid them side by side on the rug. He took the confession note and the envelope with Anthony Perotta's name on it and laid them beside the tickets. He laid the piece of paper on which he'd typed with McCreery's portable typewriter beside the confession. He laid them all out in a straight line across the floor and he stood there looking down at them.

A question seeped into my half-numb brain.

"How did McCreery know you were going to the Burton woman's apartment?" I asked.

Singer paused. He took quite a while to answer.

"That," he said, "is an important question."

There was a knock at the door. Big Red looked at Singer, who nodded. Big Red went over and opened the door. There was a guy there. It was Mr. Moynahan.

CHAPTER XIV

He came into the room and looked us over.

"My God," he said hoarsely. "What happened to you?"

"We had some differences of opinion," Singer said, "with the occupant of this apartment."

"I understood this was where I could find a man named McCreery, a detective."

"It was," I said. "Mr. McCreery has departed."

Moynahan glanced around the room.

"I—after you told me that Mr. Angora was dead," he said, "I got worried. It puts me in a hell of an embarrassing situation."

"I should think so," I said.

"Well, I thought—there's a chance, a slight chance, that I might be able to get some private detective to go to work and find the money, or at least the culprit."

"How did you come to pick McCreery?" I asked.

"McCreery has done some investigating for the insurance company that protects the Spark-EE Corporation. I knew of him. Never met him. He seemed like the logical man to go to. I called him earlier and made an appointment with him. He said he'd be here now."

"He left in kind of a hurry," I said.

Singer was studying the objects on the floor. He seemed to have forgotten about Moynahan. I went back through the bedroom into the bathroom and got a drink of water. Moynahan followed me.

"If you don't mind," he said, "just who are you two fellows?"

"It's a long story," I said. "Singer Batts is a scholar. On the side he dabbles in criminology—against his will. I work for him."

"You're a scholar too?"

"No. I manage the hotel."

"Oh, I see."

He didn't look as if he saw. He looked as if none of it made any sense.

"Is it on the level, about Angora?" he asked.

"It appears to be on the level," I said.

"How did you find him?"

"Well, nobody answered the door when we knocked, so we went in and looked around. We found him—what was left of him—down in the cellar."

We went back into the living room.

"You might like to read the confession of Antonio Perotta," Singer said, handing it to Moynahan.

Moynahan sat down and read it.

"I can't believe it," he said, shaking his head. "Antonio Perotta. He was a good man, a hard worker."

Singer was gathering up the other exhibits, stuffing them into his pockets.

"It's one o'clock in the morning," he said. "Joseph is wounded and I am not in the best of condition myself. If you will excuse us, we'll get some sleep. I imagine you're welcome to wait until Mr. McCreery gets back."

"Yes," Moynahan said. "I think I will. You understand my position, of course."

"Of course," Singer said. "I trust you will find a solution in a hurry."

"So do I," Moynahan said.

We went out and got in the car, Big Red in the back seat. I had started the motor when the green sedan pulled up alongside of us and Angelo got out.

"McCreery was in town when Marcella got it," he said.

"So," Singer said.

"Nick Andrews is in the tank," Angelo said.

I looked at him.

"The cops got him?"

"He got turned in to the cops."

"By whom?" Singer asked.

"By McCreery."

There was some silence.

"I think we'll spring him out of there," Angelo said.

I liked it better to think of him being in jail. It seemed safer in jail. I couldn't figure out why McCreery wanted him there, but then I couldn't figure out much of anything.

Singer's eyes fastened on Angelo's, caught and held them. Angelo blinked without looking away.

"I have a message for Caesar Fortunata," Singer said. "I know positively that Nick Andrews did not kill the Cipriano sisters. I will explain this to Mr. Fortunata at the earliest possible moment. Meanwhile, since Nick Andrews is in a relatively safe place, I would prefer that he be left there."

Angelo stared at him.

"In escrow, so to speak," Singer said.

"You will see Mr. Fortunata?" Angelo said.

"I will," Singer said.

Angelo continued to stare at him for a couple of minutes. Then he took his hands off the car door and stood away from it.

"I'll tell him," he said.

He got into the green sedan and drove away.

"He turned into quite a gold mine," I said. "I take back the mean things I said about him."

"I'm sure he's well disciplined," Singer said. "I would not choose him for a partner in anything but crime."

"What does Fortunata want with Nick anyway?" I asked.

"A life was taken—two lives—two lives named Cipriano. A life must be taken in exchange. Nick was selected."

I kept quiet.

"We were given thirty-six hours," Singer said slowly. "It will be a simple matter for Fortunata to get his hands on Nick when the time is up."

"Where are we going?" I said.

"To the Angora house, Joseph, to meet Doctor Sandefur."

From the back seat, Big Red said, "I wish I knew what was going on."

"I'll write a book about it," I said, "and send you a copy."

"I can't read your books," he said.

"All right. Then I'll send you some pictures."

"What about the kid, Nick?" he said.

"We'll get some lawyer to spring him," I said. "We'll get Perry Mason."

"Who's Perry Mason?"

"Some lawyer."

"I guess I don't know him."

"I'll send you a book about him. You can read that all right. Eighty-five million other people can."

"What you doing?" Big Red asked. "Selling books for him or something?"

"Not exactly. I guess it's more the other way around."

I pulled up and stopped in front of the Angora house.

CHAPTER XV

There was a guy sitting on the front steps.

"That is Doctor Sandefur," Singer said, as we got out of the car. "He is a noted archaeologist with a criminal hobby—I don't mean that exactly."

"He digs things up out of holes in the ground?" Big Red asked.

"Yes," Singer said.

Doctor Sandefur didn't look as if he could dig much of a hole. He was about five-feet-four, weight around ninety-eight pounds. He wore a pince-nez with a black ribbon and he spoke with an effeminate voice.

"I had begun to wonder," he said to Singer, "whether this was the right place."

"I'm sorry we're late," Singer said.

"Where are these bones?" Doctor Sandefur asked.

"Inside. In the basement," Singer said.

We all went inside.

Everything was the same as it had been before. The dust lay thick all over. The light switches didn't work. The street light shone dimly into the rooms and the cellar door was closed. I had brought the flashlight from the car this time so we wouldn't have to light matches. Singer went first, then Big Red, then Doctor Sandefur, then me. We climbed down the stairs to the moist basement and found our way to the furnace.

Doctor Sandefur went right to work on the pile of bones. He laid them all out in position, while I held the light. When he got through he had what looked like a pretty complete skeleton.

He stood up and looked at it, tapping his chin with his pince-nez. He walked around it slowly, looking at it from all angles. He got down on his knees and studied the skull at close range.

"Where did you find it?" he asked.

Singer pointed to the hole in the wall. Doctor Sandefur took the flashlight and peered into the hole. He stayed there quite a while. He began to mutter to himself, but I couldn't catch what he said. It sounded like a foreign language.

Then he came back and knelt again beside the skeleton.

"I'll have to take him to the lab and run a few tests," he said. "What can we put him in?"

It sounded like a very informal way to discuss something that had once been alive.

Singer looked at me.

"I've got a couple of gunny sacks in the back of the car," I said.

"A gunny sack will do nicely," Doctor Sandefur said.

I went out to the car and got one and brought it back. Doctor Sandefur leaned down, picked up the bones and dropped them into the sack. When he had finished, he pulled the open end together in his fist and slung it over his shoulder.

"By the way," he said to Singer, "who is this?"

"This was a man named Charles Angora," Singer said.

"Has his discovery been reported to the police?"

"Not to my knowledge," Singer said.

"Hmm," Doctor Sandefur said.

He looked at Big Red, then he looked at me. I had done some limping getting into and out of the Angora basement.

"Get yourself shot, young man?" he asked.

"I did," I said. "Right in the tibia."

"Indeed?" he said. "Then it certainly does you no good to limp in such a way as to favor your femur."

"Then I got shot in the femur," I said. "What the hell. Shot one way or the other."

Suddenly he laughed, a light, high laugh.

"All right, Singer," he said. "I would not take the risk for anyone else. But, if the thing should ever come up, I know you wouldn't bother to mention that Doctor Rudolph Sandefur had anything to do with finding the skeleton."

"Naturally not," Singer said.

"It will take me the rest of the night," the doctor said, "to run the tests. I'll have some sort of answer for you early in the morning."

"Thank you," Singer said.

Doctor Sandefur went quickly up the stairs, the gunny sack dangling from his shoulder. We followed him. Outside we said good night and Singer and Big Red and I got in the car.

"We will get some sleep now?" I asked.

"Yes," Singer said. "I need time to think before confronting Fortunata."

"You know the answer now?" I asked.

"I know part of it," Singer said. "I will know the rest of it within the next few hours."

I didn't question him further. If he said he knew, he knew. I knew he wouldn't sleep himself, but I knew I had to get some for me or die on my feet.

We went back to the hotel and went up to Nick's room. Big Red called a doctor he knew and the doctor came in to fix my leg. He gave me a hypodermic and probed around in there for a while and I wished he'd given me more of that needle. He put a new dressing on the wound and gave me some penicillin and wrote out a prescription.

"Better stay off it for a few days," he said.

"Oh, sure."

"Do the best you can," he said.

He started to go out.

"It's a gunshot wound," I said.

"Yes, I saw it was," he said.

"Don't you care how it happened?"

"You want to keep talking about it?" he said.

"All right," I said and shut up. I don't know what made me so talkative anyway. It must have been the drug he'd given me.

But in the next thirty seconds, the treatment had another effect. It put me to sleep. A moment before I drifted off, I saw Singer sitting at the little table. He had the confession note, the airline reservations and the faded envelope spread out in front of him. He stared at them. He got out a pencil and a piece of paper and started to write.

He was still writing when I woke up. It was eleven-thirty in the morning. There were heavy black circles under Singer's eyes. I saw that he had quite a pile of papers there with his big, scrawly handwriting all over them. I watched him while he shuffled through them, finally laid the pencil down, folded the papers together and put them in his pocket.

"Doctor Sandefur called," he said, knowing I was awake, although he hadn't turned to look. "He said, strictly off the record, as he put it, that Charles Angora died not later than 1940. Not later than 1940 and certainly not earlier than 1937."

"Oh," I muttered, trying to wake all the way up. "That's a big spread. No insurance company would pay off on that evidence."

"No," Singer said, "and it is an insurance company we must call on."

"Right now?"

"After you have risen from your bed and after we have seen Mr. Fortunata."

"Then there's no hurry," I said.

"Of course not," he said. "But I would like to be at Mr. Fortunata's residence within half an hour."

So I hurried. I might have known.

We made pretty good time. We stood at the iron grille outside Fortunata's apartment at eleven-fifty-five. The ape man went over us again for guns and we met the Filipino boy again and he showed us right in.

Fortunata stood by the window, posing this time in a yellow dressing gown with a black dragon and with bright yellow slippers. His lined, cruel face was flat and exhausted, as if it had fallen in the water and he had picked it out and wrung it dry.

"Well?" he said to Singer.

"I told Angelo I would call on you."

"Why?" Fortunata said.

"To explain that Nick Andrews was in no way responsible for the death of the Cipriano sisters."

"You think that means anything to me?"

"It means something to Nick Andrews."

Fortunata turned and crossed the room. He stopped over there, turned again and walked back to look at Singer.

"What strange power do you have, Mr. Batts," he asked, his voice thin and deadly, "that you can cause my men to forget themselves so far? What did you do to Angelo that caused him to lose sight of Nick Andrews? How could that happen?"

Singer looked at Fortunata for a long time. He glanced at me as if he were trying to tell me something with his eyes. But I didn't get it. I was thinking about my sore leg with the hole in it.

"Angelo is not himself," Singer said, "as you ought to know."

Fortunata nodded. I would have said that if it were possible for him to look sad, he looked sad at that moment.

"I know," he said. "And you don't help."

"Is Angelo here now?" Singer asked.

Fortunata waited a while. He seemed to be thinking something over.

"He's here."

"I'd like to speak to him," Singer said.

Fortunata moved across the room and pulled the bell rope. The door opened in the far wall and Angelo came through it. He looked at us, at Fortunata, and then he looked down at the rug.

"How much did you know about the embezzlement from the Spark-EE Corporation?" Singer asked.

Angelo's eyes flickered toward Fortunata. Fortunata glanced at him and nodded.

"I knew about Antonio Perotta," Angelo said. "I knew he was Marcella's brother-in-law. I knew he put away a lot of dough. When Marcella's sister came I knew somebody was putting the heat on her for the money. When this punk kid, Constancia's husband, came, I knew he was in on it."

"You were wrong," Singer said.

Angelo just shrugged.

"Did you know about the confession Antonio Perotta signed?" Singer asked.

"No," Angelo said.

"Did you know it involved Marcella?"

"She had nothing to do with it!" Angelo said. His voice was hot.

"Antonio Perotta said she did. He said he was in love with Marcella."

Fortunata had been standing with his back to us. Now he turned slowly and stared first at Singer, then at Angelo.

Angelo began to curse, slowly, softly, in Italian. After a few moments Fortunata said something sharp to him in Italian and Angelo shut up.

"Mr. Batts," Fortunata said. "Tell me about the case. We will see what we think."

Singer looked at Fortunata and his face hardened a little. He had talked very gently to Angelo, the way he might talk to somebody around Preston, some old friend. Now his voice had an edge on it.

"Somebody began to embezzle certain funds of the Spark-EE Corporation," Singer said. "The Spark-EE Corporation paid a huge royalty monthly to the inventor of the beverage, a Charles Angora. A member of the firm was employed to deliver the royalty periodically, in cash. One night, the delivery boy found Mr. Angora dead. It occurred to him that if he could hide the body of Angora, there was no reason why he shouldn't continue to deliver the money each month and pocket the cash himself. It would be simple enough to forge a receipt."

"Antonio Perotta did this?" Fortunata asked.

"Yes. When it appeared he was to be drafted into the service, he made arrangements with his wife, Constancia, to take the money he had stolen thus far and put it in a safe place. He also made arrangements to continue the embezzlement, through a confederate, with a regular payment to Constancia, as the deliveries were made."

"That's right!" Angelo said suddenly. Fortunata looked at him and he looked down at the rug again.

"The confederate continued in Antonio's footsteps, sending a share of the money to Constancia. But then Antonio Perotta was killed in action. And by this time the confederate wanted to stop the embezzlement. It had worked well up to this point. Now, it would be dangerous to continue it. But, unfortunately, he couldn't just stop. Because Constancia would have missed getting the money and she would have been reminded of what Antonio had told her, about the letter exposing the confederate, the letter that Antonio had hidden along with the corpse of Charles Angora in the house on Bellevue Place."

"What is this letter?" Fortunata asked.

"It is very simple," Singer said. "In order to insure that the confederate would continue the embezzlement and continue to send the payment to Constancia, he arranged to hold a threat of exposure over the confederate's head. He informed the confederate of the letter—perhaps even let him read it—but he did not tell him where it was hidden. He told Constancia of the existence of the letter, but he didn't tell her where it was hidden either."

"And the letter—what was in it?" Fortunata asked.

"You may read it," Singer said.

He handed Antonio Perotta's confession message to Fortunata, who read it carefully. When he had finished he handed it to Angelo. Angelo read it, crumpled it in his hand and threw it on the floor. Singer leaned down, picked it up, smoothed it out and put it back in his pocket.

"It's not true," Angelo said. "Marcella didn't know anything about it, except what Antonio Perotta did. She didn't know where it was. She knew Antonio took the money and that he gave it to Constancia. She knew somebody was after Constancia. She thought it was to get the money. She didn't know nothing about the letter!"

It was the longest speech I had ever heard Angelo make. Fortunata was staring at him. There was a long pause.

"This confederate," Fortunata said. "Who is he? Or she?"

"I don't know," Singer said.

"It would have to be somebody who worked for the Spark-EE Corporation," Fortunata said.

Singer started to answer, then paused.

"Not necessarily," he said.

"Why not?" Fortunata asked.

"Has it occurred to you to wonder," Singer said, "how it would be possible for a man to die, to be buried in his own house for at least eight years, and to call forth no inquiry, even from his nearest neighbors?"

An impatient look twisted Fortunata's face.

"All right," he said. "Explain it to me. You are doing the talking, Mr. Batts."

"In a city," Singer said patiently, "people are not inclined to pry into the household affairs of their neighbors, except in extreme emergencies or in cases of obvious irregularity. That is to say, if Charles Angora's next-door neighbor happened to see his corpse lying on the front porch, he might at least call the police. If he saw the windows dark, night after night, eventually get broken and never replaced, saw continuous calls by representatives of the utilities, newsboys and so on, he might get suspicious enough to take a look for himself. But if he merely failed to see Mr. Angora in person outside his house, if some semblance, even a meager semblance, of normal life were maintained around the place, he would stay away, he would ask no questions."

"Yes, yes," Fortunata said, sighing.

"That semblance of normal life was maintained," Singer said. "There was a person who went to the Angora house regularly, who carried in the papers, arranged now and then to have the broken windows replaced, who paid the utility bills, and, incidentally, who signed the receipts for the payments to Charles Angora."

"Who?" Fortunata asked.

"I don't know. Perhaps it was Marcella Cipriano."

Angelo moved forward in a catlike spring. I tripped him. Fortunata helped him up and said something to him in Italian. Angelo subsided.

"But I know," Singer said, "that it was not Nick Andrews. I know that Nick Andrews had nothing to do with the embezzlement, that he knew nothing of it, that he didn't even know his wife had that money, until Marcella Cipriano gave it to him in her apartment when she let him get away from Angelo."

"She didn't do that!" Angelo said. "He hit her in the head and took a powder."

"He hit her in the head at her request," Singer said. "She was afraid of what might happen to him. She was more frightened of you than of the police."

"Naturally," Fortunata said. "How can you be so sure, Mr. Batts, that the Andrews boy did not kill his wife and sister-in-law?"

"For some very clear reasons," Singer said. "For one thing, the confession note you just read is obviously a forgery. I find that it was composed on a typewriter belonging to a private detective named McCreery."

"Him," Angelo said.

"There is no reason in the world to suppose that Nick Andrews had any access to that typewriter...

"There is the fact of the manner in which the murders were committed. When Constancia was killed, Nick was out of the city. He returned to find the deed done. I have more than his word for this. I have a logical progression of other facts that lead up to it, that run through it and that continue after it was done."

"So," Fortunata said.

"Constancia was killed because the murderer thought she either had on her person or knew the whereabouts of the letter that should have been in this envelope, the letter that was replaced by the false confession you have read. The murderer tried once to elicit this information from her in Washington. Constancia fled to Chicago. The murderer followed up his suspicion and went to Marcella's apartment, still in search of the letter. Either he was surprised by Constancia in the course of his search, or he merely killed her in order to give himself time to search."

"Yes?" Fortunata said.

"Marcella was killed for much the same reason, except that by the time of her death the murderer's desperation had increased. During his second search, he went through Marcella's apartment in a very thorough manner. I have a witness who saw the search with her own eyes."

Fortunata's eyes gleamed.

"You have?"

"Yes," Singer said. "Even if you fail to grant that Nick Andrews is cleared in the case of Constancia's death, you will have to admit that he could not have conducted the search on the night of Marcella's murder. He was with my partner, Joe Spinder, for the entire evening."

Fortunata looked at me.

"Mr. Spinder, of course," he said, "is telling the truth."

"Of course," Singer said. "It doesn't matter whether you believe it to be the truth. The truth in this case is absolute."

"And how did the suitcase full of money come into Nick Andrews' hands?" Fortunata asked.

"Marcella gave him the money," Singer said.

"He hit her in the head and took the money and took a powder," Angelo said stubbornly.

Singer looked at Angelo for a while.

"I have a complete description of the appearance of Marcella Cipriano's body," Singer said. "If she had been struck on the head hard enough to knock her out completely, there would have been some sign of it two days later. There was no sign. Nick Andrews merely tapped her lightly—reluctantly—in accordance with her instructions."

Angelo looked down at the floor.

"What do you want of me?" Fortunata asked.

"Angelo informs us that Nick is in the hands of the police," Singer said. "I want your help in gaining his release."

"How can I help you?" Fortunata asked. "It is the police who are holding him. Not I."

"Has the death of Constancia Andrews been reported to the police?" Singer asked.

"I don't know," Fortunata said.

"How was her body disposed of?"

"I wouldn't know that either, Mr. Batts."

Singer gave Fortunata a long look.

"You refuse to assist me in obtaining the release of Nick Andrews?"

"Let me think about it," Fortunata said.

"I will be in the office of Lieutenant Morgan within the hour," Singer said. "I will have Lieutenant Morgan get in touch with you."

"I don't know a Lieutenant Morgan," Fortunata said.

"You must have known him at one time, well enough to insist that the murder of Marcella Cipriano be listed as a suicide."

"That was a routine precaution," Fortunata said. "Besides, I have no dealings with the lower officers. I would have operated on another level."

"Very well," Singer said. "You will hear from me again." He walked to the door. I followed him, dragging my bad leg. Nobody said anything. Nobody came after us. We went outside and to the elevator and down to the street.

"To the office of the Northwestern Casualty Company on Wacker Drive near Michigan," Singer announced.

We went there.

CHAPTER XVI

We went to the office of Mr. Ezra Prickett, Examiner. It was a bare office on the ninth floor with a frosted glass door and a drinking fountain just outside. Mr. Prickett was in his shirt sleeves. He was a heavy-set man and he was perspiring freely. He took off his glasses when we went in.

"My name is Singer Batts," Singer said. "This is Joseph Spinder. You have been informed of the embezzlement from the Spark-EE Corporation?"

"Informed!" Mr. Prickett said. "I have been everything but accused! How in the name of God such a thing could go on so long and come to such a hideous figure... Excuse me, gentlemen. What do you know about this Spark-EE Corporation?"

Singer told him. He told him everything he'd told Fortunata, except that he didn't mention Marcella Cipriano. Mr. Prickett sat and listened.

"I never saw you before," he said to Singer. "How do you fit in here? What do you want?"

Singer sighed. "I have been asked that question before."

"It's a natural question," Mr. Prickett said. "Tell me the facts. Who is this confederate you mentioned? Who committed the murders? Why aren't the police working on it? Why wasn't I told?"

"I can't answer all those questions," Singer said. "I think it may be possible for me to arrange to restore some of the stolen funds."

Now it was Prickett's turn to sigh.

"I might have guessed," he said. "What's the deal?"

"That is for you to say," Singer said.

"How much can you restore? Mind you—I said nothing about immunity or anything like that."

"I require no immunity," Singer said. "On the other hand, I don't require money either. But, just for the sake of discussion—how much would you give for a partial restitution?"

Mr. Prickett shifted around in his chair and perspired some more.

"How do I know? How much of it can you restore?"

"I can't restore any of it," Singer said. "I said that I might be able to arrange for a partial restitution."

"How much?"

Prickett was about to fall out of his chair.

"Say, two hundred thousand dollars."

Prickett did some rapid mental computation.

"That would be about one-half of the total amount. We would be glad to reimburse you for your time and trouble."

"To what extent?" Singer asked.

Mr. Prickett squirmed some more. Finally he said, "On a percentage basis—say one percent."

"Two thousand dollars—it hardly seems—"

"Five percent," Mr. Prickett said.

"Understand me, Mr. Prickett," Singer said, "I am not bargaining. It is necessary that I know how far you can go. Whether or not I can make the arrangement depends on whether I can make the offer sound attractive."

Prickett finally exploded. He huffed and puffed and bounced around in his chair and got up and ran out to the fountain and mopped his face and sat down and chewed the end off a cigar and lit it.

"I can't talk business until I see the money," he said. "How do I know you didn't steal it from somebody else?"

I laughed.

"What's so funny?" he said, glaring at me.

"You're talking to Singer Batts," I said to him quietly.

"It doesn't mean a thing to me," Prickett said.

"All right," I said, "but you'll never forget it."

Singer stood up.

"I must go," he said. "If I could arrange to restore part of the money, would you pay, say, as much as ten percent as a reward?"

"Twenty thousand dollars?"

"It might be a choice between recovering a hundred and eighty thousand or nothing at all."

"If it came to that—" Prickett said, "we might bargain. That's the best I can say. We might bargain."

"Thank you," Singer said.

We started out.

"Wait!" Prickett came up out of the chair again. "Where can I get in touch with you?"

"Well," Singer said slowly, "for the next half-hour, you can get in touch with me through Lieutenant Morgan of the homicide department of your city police."

Prickett scribbled on a pad. While he scribbled, we left.

"Lieutenant Morgan is next?" I said.

"Yes, Joseph."

"You ought to go in some business," I said. "You've got the head for it."

"The head is a sorry tool without the heart," Singer said. "I have no heart for this work."

We started out through a revolving door. I bumped into somebody. My bad leg threw me off balance and I found myself with my nose buried in this big guy's chest. I stepped back.

"Mr. Moynahan," I said. "Excuse me."

"Hello," he said vaguely. "I was on my way up to the insurance company."

He carried a couple of big ledgers under his arm.

"You have checked back over your books?" Singer asked.

"I have," Mr. Moynahan said. "I would never have believed Antonio Perotta capable of such a thing. But I have it here in black and white."

"Do you have a moment to tell me what you've found?" Singer said.

"Well—" Mr. Moynahan said, "in an hour or so, the police will be working. I hardly think we need—"

"I should like very much to know what you've found," Singer said. "The police will have a long road to travel. I might be able to help them."

"Well—" he glanced into the building, then back at Singer. "Come along," he said. "We'll sit down here in the lobby."

We sat down, side by side, on a wooden bench and Moynahan opened the biggest of his ledgers. I glanced at it, but it didn't mean a thing to me. There were a few words and a lot of figures. I couldn't read the words and the figures were just numbers.

"You can see," Moynahan explained to Singer, "how we set the royalty payments up. We have a column here in the journal for accounts payable, a column for accounts paid and two columns for dates. Accounts payable are entered in the journal daily and when they are paid, an entry is made in the opposite column, and this entry is also dated."

"I see," said Singer, and I guess he did.

"The royalties due Angora were entered like the rest of accounts payable, at a given date. This date was different each month, according to the date of our completion of the monthly balance sheet. It might, conceivably, fall on the same date in March as in, say, October. But month by month it would vary, between the 10th and 20th of the month.

"That is important to remember."

"Yes," Singer said. "I presume the payments of the royalty would vary in much the same way."

"Yes. There would be a stretch of a few days during which we would make up the cash tab for the royalties, send for the cash, put it in the office safe and deliver it. The chance that the actual payment would fall on the same day each month for more than two months in a row—and only in February and March, probably—that chance would be infinitesimal."

"I understand," Singer said.

"Yet," Mr. Moynahan said, "beginning late in 1941, that is exactly what began to happen."

Singer gazed at him.

"You mean that at that time, the payments to Angora began to be entered on the same day each month?"

"That is just what I mean. It started in November 1941, six months after Antonio Perotta came to work for us. It continued until he was drafted into the service. It is unreasonable. It is so unlikely that it is almost impossible to believe. But I have the evidence right in front of me. It is almost as incredible to realize that Antonio would slip up on such a point."

"But you told us," Singer said, "that you have continued to pay the royalties, ever since Antonio Perotta went to war."

Mr. Moynahan heaved a deep sigh.

"Yes, we have," he said. "I don't know what arrangements were made. I don't know who has been receiving the stolen money. But I know that it has been worked out by whomever was helping Antonio."

After a moment Singer said, "You'll want to be getting along to see Mr. Prickett."

"Yes," Moynahan said, standing up.

"Did you get in touch with Mr. McCreery?" Singer asked.

"No," Moynahan said. "He never came back. I meant to ask you—how did you come to be there?"

"It's a long story," Singer said. "I will try to tell it to you some day when we have more time."

"Thanks for your interest in the case," Moynahan said. "If it hadn't been for you, I would probably have kept on okaying those tabs till the cows came home."

Singer laughed gently.

"I'm glad to have been of some service," Singer said.

"Will you be going home now?"

"Not yet," Singer said. "I have yet to uncover the murderer of the Cipriano girls."

"Oh, yes. Well, I'll look forward to seeing you again," Moynahan said and disappeared across the lobby.

We went back out to the street.

"And now?" I said.

"We will visit Lieutenant Morgan," Singer said, "and try to get Nick out of jail."

I drove to City Hall. We climbed the stairs to the lieutenant's office. I knocked on the door and somebody said, "Come in."

A plainclothesman sat in a chair by the window. Lieutenant Morgan sat at his desk. He looked up when we walked in.

"You keep turning up," he said. "I thought you went home."

"I went part way," I said.

"Your name is Singer Batts?" he asked.

Singer nodded.

"I've heard of you," the lieutenant said. "What's on your mind?"

"You may recall," Singer said, "that Joe called you yesterday and told you Constancia Cipriano had been murdered."

The lieutenant's face went blank. "I don't recall," he said.

"Nevertheless," Singer said, "it's true."

"So?" the lieutenant said.

"Constancia Cipriano was the wife of Nick Andrews, whom you now have in custody."

The lieutenant looked puzzled.

"I want him released," Singer said.

The lieutenant turned and looked at the detective. The detective shook his head.

"We're not holding any Nick Andrews," the lieutenant said.

"When did you let him go?" Singer asked.

"We never held him. What are you talking about? When were we supposed to pick him up?"

Singer looked nonplussed—a rare look on him.

"I understood," he said, "that McCreery had turned him in to you."

"McCreery. Pat McCreery—that shamus? He wouldn't turn anybody in to us."

"This is true?" Singer said.

"So help me," the lieutenant said. "I never even heard of this Nick Andrews."

"You would have," I said, "if you'd investigated the murder of Constancia Cipriano."

The lieutenant sighed. "Mr. Batts—" he said, "you are a detective—what they call a brilliant amateur detective. I am just a cop—professional."

"That is true," Singer said.

"That does not mean I am any smarter than you. It just means I've got a job to do in a certain way. You can do anything you want to."

Singer looked innocent and puzzled.

"You say a girl was murdered. All right, I've checked into it. I say she committed suicide—just like her sister, Marcella."

"But, Lieutenant—" Singer began.

The telephone rang. The lieutenant picked it up.

"Hello…" he said. "Yeah?…yeah?"

He listened for quite a while. His eyes shifted, came to rest on Singer's face. Finally he said, "Sure. Right away."

He hung up slowly.

"I'm sorry about this, Mr. Batts," he said. "But I'm forced to put you under arrest."

Singer took it calmly.

"On what charge?" he asked.

The lieutenant wasn't quite ready for this. He turned to the cop at the window.

"Is there any kind of a charge that has to do with 'guilty knowledge'?" he asked.

"I don't know," the cop said. "I find 'em—I don't try 'em."

"That would have been Mr. Prickett of Northwestern Casualty?" Singer said.

"He's on his way down to swear out a warrant," the lieutenant said. "I'm sorry, my hands are tied."

"Like they were tied after Constancia Cipriano was murdered?" I said.

"Aw, shut up," he said.

Singer was thinking it over.

"Is there any such thing as constitutional rights?" he asked.

Lieutenant Morgan's eyes came suddenly alert. He studied Singer's face.

"Maybe," he said.

"I want to make a telephone call," Singer said.

The lieutenant glanced at the cop. The cop just looked out the window. Finally Lieutenant Morgan reached out and pushed his desk phone across to Singer. Singer lifted it and the switchboard girl said something.

"You will be able, I'm sure," Singer said to her, "to find the telephone number of Caesar Fortunata. You will be good enough to get him on the phone and tell him that Mr. Singer Batts is calling."

Lieutenant Morgan studied his fingernails. The cop studied Lieutenant Morgan. Singer waited at the telephone.

It took less time than I would have expected. There were some clicks in the telephone and finally Singer said, "Mr. Fortunata, this is Singer Batts. I am in the office of Lieutenant Morgan of the homicide squad. Angelo, for once, was misinformed. Nick Andrews is not being held by the police... Yes. But I am now under arrest myself and if I am to find Nick Andrews— and Marcella's murderer—it is necessary that I get out of here without delay. Will you speak to Lieutenant Morgan?"

Singer handed the phone to the lieutenant. The lieutenant took it and said, "Yeah?"

Then there was quite a pause while the lieutenant listened. Little by little as he listened, a look of intense hatred came into his face. I had never seen any hatred quite so concentrated in one man's face before, and quite suddenly I understood the lieutenant as I would never have understood him if this had not happened.

He listened for a long time and finally he said, "Yeah," shortly, with the hate underneath the tone, and he hung up.

"All right," he said softly, looking at the top of his desk. "All right, Mr. Batts," he said. "You may go."

Singer and I got up. The lieutenant was staring down at his desk.

"Thank you," Singer said.

The lieutenant looked up. "When you see Caesar Fortunata," he said, "you can tell him something for me. Tell him the day will come. I don't know when or how, but the day will come."

Singer's voice was warm. "I'm sure it will, Lieutenant," he said. "And I wish you good luck."

We walked out of the lieutenant's office and went down to the car.

"What happened to Nick?" I asked.

"I'm not sure. But I am sure that we must act rapidly."

"I don't see what McCreery would want with him."

"Mr. McCreery," Singer said, "is laboring under a large delusion. The delusion that Nick Andrews knows where more of the embezzled money can be found."

"More?"

"At least again as much," Singer said, "as we hold in a suitcase in the Preston bank. Drive to the apartment of Mrs. White."

"You going to disturb that poor, scared woman again?"

"Unfortunately," Singer said.

We had to ring the bell a long time before she came and when she did, wearing a long, quilted bathrobe that hung at a crazy angle from her thin shoulders, she started blazing away with both barrels.

"You dare come back here to pester me—it's taking advantage—just because my husband isn't home."

"Not home yet?" Singer asked.

She broke down then all at once and began to cry.

Singer patted her shoulder awkwardly.

"Now, now," he said. "I only stopped by for a moment to ask why you didn't tell us the whole truth the other night."

She turned off the tears the way you turn off the faucet.

"What do you mean?" she asked.

"You didn't tell me you saw a woman in the apartment of the murdered girl."

"I didn't see any woman," she said. "I saw a man. Two men."

"That's what you said before."

"You think I lied to you?"

"I think you just failed to tell the complete truth. From fear... Well, Mrs. White, you have nothing to fear, not from me or from the police. I know that you were not over there yourself. But I think somebody else was over there and I think you saw her."

She struggled with it for a while, but she didn't have much tenacity.

"All right," she said dully. "I saw somebody else—a woman. I was afraid to tell you after you said something about the girl being murdered by a jealous wife."

"What did the woman look like?" Singer asked.

Mrs. White's voice was bitter, with the bitterness of the plain, hard-working housewife toward the glamor girl of office, night club and call house.

"She looked like the one who got killed, only older," Mrs. White said.

"Had you ever seen her before?"

"A few times. She's lived over there a long time. I don't know what her name is."

"Where have you seen her?"

"Well—this will probably sound silly. I don't quite believe it myself, but I've seen it."

"We have a measure of honest credulity," Singer said. "Give us a chance."

"I've seen her come out of the apartment, late at night, out the back way, dressed as a scrubwoman."

I must have blinked or something.

"See," Mrs. White said. "I told you you wouldn't believe it."

"Nobody has refused to believe it," Singer said. "You have seen her dressed as a scrubwoman, leaving the apartment?"

"Yes. I'm sure she was the one."

"Why do you suppose anybody would do that?" Singer said.

"I don't know," Mrs. White said. "I don't know why a girl like that would do it. She certainly wouldn't have to."

"How often would you say you have seen her like this?"

"Not often. Maybe once a month, something like that."

"And you saw her the night in question, the other night when the young lady was murdered?"

"Yes. She came into the apartment first. The big man came in later and when he went out the woman went out too. The second man came later."

"I see. Thank you very much," Singer said.

He stood up and so did I.

"Good afternoon," Singer said, with deep understanding. "Thank you again, Mrs. White."

We walked down the hall and outside.

"Well," I said, "she came through all right. Who was the woman?"

"I dislike making hasty assumptions."

"Oh. Are we now, by any chance, going to call on Mrs. Burton?"

"Yes, Joseph."

"She won't like it."

"That is unfortunate. Perhaps we can do her a service."

I wasn't so sure that our type of service was what Mrs. Burton needed.

CHAPTER XVII

It was three-thirty in the afternoon now, about the most pleasant part of the day. The sun was shining, and if it hadn't been for my dragging leg, I would have felt good. The doctor was right. Better I should stay off it.

We went to Mrs. Burton's apartment.

No negligee this time. She was fully dressed in a smart business suit with an orchid on her lapel. She looked mighty good. She may have been, as Angelo said, "a wrong twist," but she knew how to make you like it.

I didn't seem to mean a thing to her but her eyes clouded as she looked at Singer.

"Well?" she said.

"I would like to talk to you," Singer said pleasantly.

"About what?"

"About the embezzlement perpetrated against the Spark-EE Corporation."

"I don't know anything about it."

Over in the corner were a couple of pieces of bright new luggage. A well-tailored spring coat lay across the davenport.

"You found your plane reservations?" Singer asked pleasantly.

"I never lost them," she said.

Singer gazed at her.

"Odd," he said. "What is it then that I have in my pocket?"

She looked at her watch.

"I wouldn't know," she said. "But I have my reservation in my purse."

Singer's voice hardened. "I advise you against making the trip," he said.

"Why?"

"Both you and your companion will be caught."

"How do you know I have a companion?"

"There were two reservations."

Suddenly Singer slumped. He slumped all over, starting at the head and working down to the feet.

It was a typical reaction. I braced myself. He could stand only a limited amount of incidental conversation, of beating around the bush. I was sure now he had the answer to the problem. All that was left was to wrap it up and tie the knot. Mrs. Burton was playing games, and Singer—bless his heart—was fed up.

"You," he said to her, "have regularly visited an empty house on Bellevue Place, disguised as a chambermaid. There you have forged receipts in the name of Charles Angora for large sums of money. The Northwestern Casualty Company is at this moment investigating the embezzlement. They will be interested to know that you are about to fly to Mexico City."

You could see the doubt and hesitation in her face. But it was only doubt—not certainty. She knew it was all shot now. She might brazen it out for long enough to get to the airport. But sooner or later—She stepped back from the door.

"What do you want?" she asked. Her voice was husky and low.

"I want to make an offer," Singer said.

"What kind of an offer?"

"May we come in?"

"Yes," she said, looking again at her watch.

We went in and sat down.

"If you are innocent of embezzlement and murder," Singer said, "you can probably make a good deal of money—right away."

"How?" she asked.

"By giving us a statement about your assignment at the Angora house."

She looked Singer over carefully.

"I have to know how far I'm protected," she said.

"To the greatest extent possible, as far as I am able to control it," Singer said.

"Thanks for nothing," she said.

"That is the best offer I can make," Singer said. "If you did not actually commit the embezzlement yourself and if you did not murder or help to murder either or both of the Cipriano sisters, I should think you would have a good chance of staying clear."

"How can I know whether to trust you?"

"You can't know," Singer said. "You can trust."

"How do I know the insurance company will give me a cut?"

"That, too, you must take on trust. I make no guarantee."

"You know where the money is?" she asked.

"Yes," Singer said.

"Does McCreery know where it is?"

"Why do you ask?"

"What if he got there first? What if you made a deal with him too?"

"I made no deal with Mr. McCreery. Nobody can get his hands on the money without my release."

She thought it over for a while and finally she cleared her throat, re-crossed her nice legs and said, "You show me the money, and I'll talk. Not before."

"That would be inconvenient," Singer said. "The money is some two hundred miles away."

"Oh. Well, I wouldn't have time to go that far and still make the plane."

"You won't make the plane in any case," Singer said.

"Won't I?"

"No. The police will stop you."

She laughed. She threw back her pretty head and laughed loud and long. "The police!" she said. "They haven't a thing on me."

Singer sighed. "Call Lieutenant Morgan, Joseph," he said.

I went to the telephone, dialed City Hall. A girl answered.

"Lieutenant Morgan's office," I said.

Mrs. Burton was walking across the room. She reached in front of me, laid her finger on the phone and broke the connection.

"All right," she said. "You take me where the money is and we'll discuss the situation."

"What about your plane?" I said.

"I can always get another plane."

"The guy won't like to be stood up," I said.

"He won't mind when he sees the money," she said.

"Unfortunately," Singer said, "we cannot leave town until we find Nick Andrews. Possibly you could help us with that."

"No," she said.

You couldn't tell what "No" meant: whether she couldn't, or wouldn't.

Singer appeared to give up. "Very well," he sighed. "We will go. Perhaps the police can find Nick Andrews."

"I'll have to change," Mrs. Burton said.

"You look fine," I said.

"I'm dressed for a plane, not a car," she said. "This wouldn't be comfortable."

"By all means," Singer said gallantly.

She went back to the bedroom and closed the door. I didn't get any of this. I didn't know why Singer gave up on Nick so easily or why Mrs. Burton consented to go so far just on a chance of making a few thousand bucks.

Singer walked over to a coffee table in front of the davenport and picked up Mrs. Burton's purse. He took something out of it, an envelope. Then he took another envelope out of his pocket. What he had were two envelopes, identical. Inside of each were two plane reservations to Mexico City. They were clearly not duplicates. They were two distinct pairs of reservations.

"She was playing two guys against each other," I said.

"I fear so."

"I wonder which lucky fellow will win?" I said.

He shrugged. He put both sets of reservations in his pocket, closed and replaced her purse.

"What about Nick?" I asked.

"We will find Nick. At the moment I want to get this young lady out of her apartment."

We had already waited fifteen minutes. We sat around for another ten before it dawned on me. I looked at Singer.

"She's stalling," I said.

"Undoubtedly."

"Can we wait?"

"We have little choice," he said. "It is now four o'clock. The reservations are for five-thirty. The trip to the airport will require at least an hour. We have perhaps thirty minutes."

"Maybe I can hurry her up."

"Perhaps."

I went back to the bedroom door and pounded on it.

"Just a minute," she said.

"Let's go," I said.

I stood by the door, waiting. There was no sound in the room. How can you change your clothes without making a sound?

I thought I heard a noise, a light, thumping noise, muffled and dim.

The door had a keyhole. I looked at it. It was not exactly in my line of duty, but we were pressed for time. I hunched down and put my eye to it.

Mrs. Burton stood with her back to me, looking out the window, smoking a cigarette. She wore the same suit she had worn when we came in. She hadn't changed a stitch.

I kept hearing the thumping noise. It came from her clothes closet, in the far corner of the room. The closet door was closed.

Mrs. Burton heard it too. She jerked her head impatiently. She went to the bed, reached under her pillow and got that gun. Then she started toward the closet.

I couldn't have signed any affidavit as to who was in there, but I had a good strong hunch. I twisted the knob and walked into the bedroom. Mrs. Burton swung around, pointing the gun at me. I dived onto the bed, rolled across and dropped off the other side. She re-aimed and I caught her wrist and twisted as she fired.

There were sounds from the other room now, men's voices. Mrs. Burton dropped the gun and ran out there. I jerked open the closet door.

My hunch worked out. Nick Andrews lay on the closet floor, tied hand and foot, the feet drawn up behind him. A flour sack was pulled over his head and tied around his neck. His feet were bare and the bottoms of them were in bad shape. The blisters were as big as my thumb and there were a lot of them.

I crawled in there, opened my pocket knife and cut the rope that bound his hands and feet. I cut the string that held the sack around his neck. His face was as much of a mess as his feet, only not from burns. Probably from the butt of McCreery's gun.

I shook him a little and he opened his eyes, searching. It was dark in the closet.

"It's Joe," I said. "Come on—let's get out of here."

"Joe—" he whispered. "I can't walk... Broke—my legs."

I started to swear.

"Shut up!" a voice said.

I stood up and turned around. In the bedroom doorway stood our old friend, Max, McCreery's boy. He held a gun on me. I had no doubt he knew how to use it.

"Up to your old tricks," I said. "You got the red-hot pincers up your sleeve?"

"Shut up," he said. "Come out of the closet."

I walked out.

"I'll be back, Nick," I said.

I don't think he heard me. I think he passed out.

Max was backing into the living room. I limped along, staring at him.

"Come on!" he said. "Walk, walk."

"You're the one who shot me," I said. "You can wait, yellow belly."

It was a schoolboy's taunt and I didn't expect it to work, to bring him up close enough for me to grapple with him.

It didn't. He just kept backing and I kept limping into the narrow hallway, past the bathroom with the closed door so I couldn't duck in there, into the living room.

In there it looked like a convention. Singer Batts sat on the davenport. Mrs. Burton stood beside the telephone table. McCreery stood in the middle of the room, holding a gun on Singer. McCreery was flanked on the right by two of the biggest boys I had ever seen. They looked like all of seven feet high and five feet wide. They just stood on flat feet, gazing at the floor. On McCreery's left was a scrawny, rat-like guy in a checked suit.

Singer gave me a wry smile.

"I miscalculated," he said. "I did not expect our caller to be named McCreery."

McCreery looked at Mrs. Burton and back to Singer. "Who did you expect?" he asked.

"It no longer matters," Singer said.

McCreery nodded to his right. One of the big beefy boys walked over and slugged Singer with the back of his hand. A little blood ran out of Singer's nose.

"Mr. McCreery asked you a question," he said.

Singer didn't answer. The big boy lifted his hand again. McCreery shook his head. "Lay off," he said. "I need him alive."

"If we're going to make the plane—" Mrs. Burton said.

McCreery snarled. "We're not making any plane," he said.

"Didn't you get the money?"

"No, baby," he said, "I didn't get the money. The only money available is in a bank in a town called Preston. We'll get that."

The telephone rang.

"Answer it," McCreery said.

Mrs. Burton picked up the phone. "Hello?... No, not yet... In about an hour..."

She started to hang up. McCreery snatched the phone out of her hand. He shouted into it.

"Hello—hello!" He jiggled the hook up and down. A woman's voice scratched through the receiver. McCreery listened. Then he hung up the phone. His eyes went over Mrs. Burton. She backed away. He went after her.

"That was the airport," he said. "You were going to run out on me—with him." His voice was deadly and low. "You cheap whore. You double-talking slut. You—"

"Pat—" she said, "listen to me—" He hit her three times. Once on the right, once on the left, once in the middle. She slumped to the floor.

I'd had enough. I opened my big mouth.

"You are the toughest boys in the world," I said, "when it comes to beating up women and children."

"Max," McCreery said.

Max moved in. I saw him coming, but there wasn't much I could do. I got to him twice in the face, but it only made him sore. He kicked me in the stomach. I doubled over and he clouted the back of my head with the gun. The first blow wasn't hard enough to put me clear out. While my mind faded slowly I heard McCreery say, "Pick up the dame. Bring the guy on the sofa. We'll get going."

Max finished his job. I went toward total slumber with a ringing in my ears and then that stopped. The rest was silence.

CHAPTER XVIII

It was hard to open my eyes. It was even harder to get up. I lay still on the floor, getting things in focus and I kept hearing this bell ring. I figured out it was the telephone. I got to my knees and crawled over there. I lifted the thing down and put it to my ear. I tried to say hello, but my voice got stuck.

"The plane's leaving in five minutes!" a man's voice said. "What's happened?"

"Your sweetheart won't be making it," I managed to say. "She's on her way to rob a bank."

I started to hang up. The voice got frantic.

"What? Who is this? What's that about a bank?"

There was something familiar about the voice, but I couldn't think hard enough to remember it.

"Like I said," I said. "A bank—she's going to knock it over. McCreery's helping her. They've got Singer Batts."

I hung up. What the hell. I should waste my precious last few minutes of life talking to a stranger who had been stood up by his girlfriend—a double-talking slut, McCreery had called her.

I heard someone moaning. I remembered about Nick. I started in there, still on my hands and knees. Then I got smart. I doubled back to the telephone, picked up the receiver and dialed operator. When she answered, I said, "Ambulance. Apartment 701." And I gave her the address.

Then I went into the bedroom, pausing briefly to soak my head in cold water in the bathroom as I passed it.

Nick was out of his head. I went back to the bathroom and got a cold towel and gave him a little treatment. He quieted some and finally he said my name.

"What did they want from you?" I asked.

"They wanted—the money."

"They knew you didn't have the money. They knew where it was."

"They thought I had more. They thought Marcella had told me where it was hidden. They tried to get me to tell them. But I couldn't. I didn't know."

"Take it easy," I said. "There's a doctor on the way."

"Joe—"

"Yeah?"

"Thanks for trying."

"I'm just getting started," I said. "We get you in the hospital and then I'm off after McCreery."

"I wonder whether McCreery killed Constancia—"

"He would be capable of it," I said. "But I don't figure these things out. Singer Batts is the brain of the party."

"Where is Singer Batts now?" he asked.

"I don't know," I said. "I'll find him."

There was a pause.

"Joe—" he said. "I wish—Constancia—" He stopped. I shook him a little, gently. He didn't say anything.

Passed out again, I thought, wishing I could do the same.

I went into the bathroom and took some more of the cold-water treatment. I was in there, wiping myself off, when two guys with white coats and a stretcher came into the hallway. I showed them where Nick was.

"Be careful," I told them. "He hurts in several places."

One of the two guys looked up at me. "Not any more," he said. "He's dead."

I dropped the towel. I walked slowly across the bedroom and looked down at the dark, huddled figure on the floor.

"Can't be—" I said.

"I'm afraid he is."

Suddenly, it made me sore. He had to die. We could just as well have skipped all this running around and mess. He was going to die anyway. What the hell. And now where was Singer Batts—?

Thinking about Singer snapped me out of it.

"I'm sorry," I said.

"How did it happen?" one of the guys said.

"It's too long to tell now," I said. "I've got to get going."

"You can't get going, bud, until after we get a statement."

"Look—" I said.

"No look," he said. "Sit down and take it easy. What happened to you? You're groggy."

"Yeah," I said.

I went into the living room and sat down on the davenport and put my head in my hands. I felt as if I wanted to tear it off and throw it out the window. My leg ached too. I sat there, thinking of all the swear words I knew. It covered a lot of territory and took a long time. I know a lot of words.

The door opened across from me. I looked up.

"Hello, Angelo," I said.

He didn't answer. Another guy came in behind him.

"Hello, Mr. Fortunata," I said.

I put my head back in my hands. I didn't see what they could do for me.

The two guys with the stretcher came out of the hallway. Nick was on it and he was covered up with a sheet. Caesar Fortunata leaned down and pulled the sheet away.

"Hey!" one of the men said.

Fortunata just looked at him.

"This is Mr. Caesar Fortunata," I said, "the greatest man in the world."

"Nick Andrews," Angelo said.

Fortunata replaced the sheet.

I started to get up. "Got to get going," I said. "Singer Batts—"

"Yes. Mr. Batts is the man I wanted to see," Caesar said.

"You'll have to make a trip," I said. "He's on his way home."

One of the men from the ambulance had a pad of paper in his hand. "I'll have to know what happened," he said.

"Shut up," Fortunata said to him. "What happened to Mr. Batts, Mr. Spinder?"

"He got kidnapped, by a private eye named McCreery. They are going to Preston. They are going to knock over the Preston bank and steal the money that was stolen from the Spark-EE Corporation."

"Does Mr. Batts know who murdered the Cipriano sisters?"

"I couldn't say," I said. "Right now I don't know whether Mr. Batts knows anything at all, consciously."

"Listen," the man with the pad said, "who is this corpse?"

"A kid named Nick Andrews," I said, "very unlucky in love."

"Where was he from?"

"Washington—" I got up. I didn't feel like going through all that again.

"Tell him to shut up," I said to Fortunata. "I'm going to Preston. You can come along or stay here. I don't care."

"Angelo," Fortunata said, "call Luigi."

Angelo went to the phone and dialed a number.

"Take the corpse and get out," Fortunata said.

"I have to get a statement—"

"Get out," Fortunata said.

They stood there a minute, looking at each other. Then they picked up the stretcher and started out.

"So long, Nick," I said. "I'm sorry."

Angelo hung up the phone.

"Mr. Spinder," Fortunata said, "is in no condition to drive. You and Ricci will drive Mr. Spinder's car. Ivo will drive Mr. Spinder and me. Luigi and the boys will come in the other car."

"You're going to Preston?" I said.

"Yes," Fortunata said. "I expect to find in Preston—wherever that is— the answer to the murders of the Cipriano girls. That is my only interest. We will go now."

He walked out. Angelo and I followed him. Fortunata walked straight and gracefully, as if he owned everything he looked at.

I guess he very nearly did.

My car was parked across the street. Angelo called the fat, swarthy driver out of the green sedan and the two of them got in my car. A taxi swung into the curb and four men got out. They all looked more or less like Angelo.

Fortunata led me to a limousine parked in front of the apartment. It looked like a boat, a long, black, beautiful boat. I climbed into the back seat with Fortunata.

My mind wasn't clear. This trip seemed like the wildest of wild-goose chases. If McCreery was going to rob the Preston bank and he was already in town, he would either have done the job by now or he would have been caught. Two or three guys like that couldn't hold up a whole town for hours. Somebody would call the sheriff.

But Fortunata had said he would go, and we were going. Fortunata's chauffeur drove the boat like an arrow, never missing a light, never getting stuck behind anybody. It was as if he were part of the car.

Between Hammond and Gary, Fortunata said something into a tube and the driver pulled up in front of a big roadside restaurant. It was just beginning to get dark and the lights had gone on a little ahead of time. My car pulled up beside us. Behind was the green sedan, full of guys. They weren't talking. They just sat, smoking cigarettes and waiting.

Angelo leaned out of my car.

"This is a four-hour trip," Fortunata said to him. "That's too long."

Angelo nodded. "We'll make it in three," he said.

"Good," Fortunata said. "Don't fall behind."

There was no more time wasted. We roared into the highway, heading east, and the driver got through Gary without braking once. I looked out the back window and saw my car and the green sedan behind us. Neither was having trouble keeping up the pace. I hoped my rings and valves would hold up for the trip. I hoped it even harder when we got on the clear highway again and the chauffeur got the needle up to eighty and held it there.

As we got farther and farther into the country, passing through lighted, familiar towns, he went even faster. I couldn't have done it. I wondered where he had learned to drive. He had to stop in a little place in Indiana to get gas. My car and the green sedan stopped too, with the motors running, and stood like impatient horses, waiting.

Back on the road, going eighty-five now to maintain our average, I said to Fortunata, "What is your big hurry to get there?"

"I have an engagement at one o'clock in the morning," he said. "I would not like to miss it."

"Oh," I said.

That was the total of our conversation during the trip. From time to time I spoke to the chauffeur through the speaking tube, giving him directions.

The rest of the time I worried about Singer Batts. If anything happened to him I knew it would be a lifetime fight between McCreery and Spinder. One or the other of us would have a short life.

The chauffeur slowed at an intersection and I picked up the tube. "Turn left at the next corner and follow the curve of the hard road," I said. Then I grabbed the handle of the door as we swung into the curve.

We were on the country road leading into Preston and we had to slow down some. There wasn't any choice. You just can't go eighty-five miles an hour on that road.

I didn't like to think of us roaring into quiet Preston at nine-thirty in the evening at this pace. Besides scaring the hell out of the townspeople, it would be a perfect warning to McCreery and his boys, and I didn't want to get caught in that crossfire. I prevailed upon the chauffeur to take it easy. Just before we got to the bridge at the west end of town, I told him to stop. I explained my thoughts to Fortunata. He finally nodded.

"We'll go straight in," I said, "and park across from the hotel. My car will turn right just after we cross the bridge and follow that alley to the first main street. Then double back down Front Street, turn right at the hotel corner and park across the street. The green sedan will go on through town, turn left at the east end and come back by the side streets and park a block north of the hotel."

"You explain it to them," said Fortunata.

I limped back and gave the directions and then returned to the limousine. I climbed in beside Fortunata and we started off again, slowly this time. Watching through the back window, I saw my car turn off into the alley. I told the chauffeur where to park across from the hotel.

We sat there for a minute. There weren't many people on the streets; a few kids up around the drugstore and a couple of old duffers sitting on a bench in front of the bank. In the bank there was the usual night light and no activity. Nobody was sitting on the steps of the hotel. Usually there was somebody, but there didn't have to be. It didn't prove anything. There were two cars with Illinois licenses parked beside us. They were both empty.

"I'll go in first," I said. "Alone. I'll give you an office when I find out what the situation is."

Fortunata nodded.

I climbed out and crossed the street to the hotel steps. I glanced through the screen door into the lobby. Jack Pritchard, the night clerk, sat there with his head resting on his hand, looking sick. On one of the leather sofas in the middle of the lobby sat the small rat-faced guy, reading a newspaper. I rattled the screen door. He put the paper down and fastened his eyes on me. I went on in. He sat still. He had one hand in the right-hand pocket of his coat. I gambled. I figured I had to. It was a better break than Russian Roulette. He might shoot me down in the lobby of the hotel or he might not. Anyway, he didn't have the gun out yet. And at the angle from which I approached him, he couldn't shoot me through his pocket.

That was all that saved me. He got the gun out fast, but I was there by that time, with my hand on his wrist. I twisted it, hard and fast, and he slid out of the chair and went to his knees. I pulled the gun out of his hand and slapped him with it. I slapped him hard about six times and left him on the floor. I put his gun in my pocket.

Jack Pritchard was staring at me, his eyes bulging. I went to the desk.

"Where are the rest of them?" I asked.

Jack leaned across the desk and whispered hoarsely. "Upstairs," he said.

"Where upstairs?"

"I don't know. They just came in and took over."

"Singer is up there too?"

"Yes, Joe."

"And the woman?"

"Yes."

"How long have they been here?"

"About half an hour."

"Just sitting up there?"

"I don't know. They made a phone call—from the phone on the third floor. They called Amos Bittner."

"Amos!"

"I listened in down here. They told Amos they were holding Singer Batts—hostage. They told him to come downtown and open the bank. They said—if he didn't come—or if he called the law—they'd—shoot Singer!"

For once, Jack and I agreed. For either of us, as for Amos Bittner and the entire population of Preston, the death of Singer Batts would be the death of all of us.

"Did Amos believe them?" I said.

"I guess so. He said he'd come down."

"So that's what they're waiting for," I said.

"What will you do, Joe?"

"I don't know yet. But I've got some boys outside. I guess they'd know what to do. You just sit there and keep quiet till I tell you something different."

I went back out to the car. I couldn't figure out how to handle it. I didn't want to waste any time. But I didn't know what would happen to Singer if we rushed them. I would have to ask the advice of that old campaigner, Caesar Fortunata.

CHAPTER XIX

The old campaigner referred me to the chauffeur, a recent graduate of the "heavy" rackets.

"What a setup!" he cried, when I'd explained it. "They got the bank president to come down and open it up for them."

"So what do we do?" I asked him.

"Let 'em go ahead," he said. "We'll catch 'em on the way out. They won't knock off your friend till they get through."

It was a comforting thought. It was the best plan we had.

The chauffeur gave me some instructions. I went diagonally across Front Street to the corner opposite the hotel. My car was parked there and Angelo sat beside the driver smoking a cigarette. The green sedan was parked a block away on the same side of the street.

I told Angelo what the chauffeur had said. He listened. He climbed out of the car and walked up the dark street to the green sedan.

While I waited for Angelo to come back, Amos Bittner drove slowly down Front Street in his black Buick. He parked in front of the bank, about half a block from Fortunata's limousine. He climbed out of his car, went up on the walk and turned to look across the street at the hotel.

Angelo came back. One by one, six men climbed out of the green sedan and went off in various directions, one down past the hotel, two of them on across the street—on the bank side—one diagonally toward our corner. A couple of others melted into a doorway a few doors from the bank.

One of them and Angelo went with me to stand in the doorway of the hardware store, directly across from the bank. Angelo leaned against the glass wall of the store front, balancing his knife on his hand. He said nothing.

I watched the wall of the hotel. After a couple of minutes a light went on in Room 324. A moment later a light went on in the adjoining room. The shades were down and I couldn't see who was in the rooms.

Amos Bittner was in his office in the front of the bank. You could see him clearly through the big plate-glass window. He sat at his desk shuffling through some papers. The window was bulletproof. But for anybody inside the bank, Amos was just a clay pigeon.

A car came roaring into town from the west. It slowed with a screech of brakes, made a U-turn and parked, bumping against the curb beyond where we stood in the doorway. A big guy climbed out of it, came walking fast in our direction.

"Mr. Moynahan," I said softly as he reached our doorway.

He stopped as if somebody had hit him with a sledge hammer. He peered into the doorway.

"Better get off the street," I said.

He recognized me. He came on into the doorway.

"That thief, McCreery," he said.

"Yeah," I said.

"What's going on?" he said.

"It's too complicated to explain now," I said. "Keep your eyes open and your head down."

"He was recommended to me as an honest investigator," he muttered. "Now I find—"

"How did you find out?" I said.

"Why—he notified me. Himself. He had the brass—"

"All right," I said. "We'll talk about it later."

The front door of the hotel opened and Singer Batts came out. With him was Max. Max had a gun. Singer walked down the hotel steps and started across the street, moving slowly, in short, awkward steps. He came under the street light and I saw why he walked that way. They had him hobbled. A heavy rope was knotted around his ankles. It was about a foot long. They'd made sure he wouldn't be able to break and run.

Three townspeople came out of the drugstore up the street and walked toward the bank. Singer and Max were in the middle of the street. I heard one of the townsmen say, "That's Singer Batts!"

"Hi, Singer," another called.

There was a pause and then the first one said, "That guy's got a gun."

"Step back out of the way," Max said. "You won't get hurt."

The three of them stood there, uncertain, looking at each other. Max shifted his gun for a moment. He fired once. One of the three on the sidewalk bent over, clutching at his leg. The other two helped him back into the shadows of the store fronts.

They would have to work fast now or they'd have the whole town out.

They did work fast. Max prodded Singer in the back and tried to hurry him. Singer hobbled along as well as possible. The hotel door opened again and McCreery's beef trust came out, the two of them walking fast across the street toward the bank. Right behind them came McCreery. He had the Burton woman by the wrist. They ran across the street and climbed into one of the Illinois cars parked near the limousine. The car backed out and moved slowly along the street, to cover the two heavies who were going into the bank.

Max led Singer up to the door of the bank. He got him placed so that he was plainly visible from inside the bank and from the street. It wasn't hard to figure out that if anything went wrong, got held up, or if there was any fuss, Max would shoot Singer on the spot. Amos Bittner, inside the bank, could see this clearly. I could see it clearly from where I stood across the street. I saw it too clearly. I thought we were licked. Any move from us and Singer Batts was finished.

On the other hand, they'd shoot him anyway as soon as they got what they wanted out of the bank. I was sure of this. I chewed my fingernails and stared and tried to think. But it was hard to think.

"So, what now?" I whispered to Angelo. "If we make a move, they kill him."

"Shut up," he said, "shut up and stand still."

Mr. Moynahan stood beside us, watching the bank. He took his handkerchief cut of his pocket and mopped his face.

The two beefy ones had gone into the bank. The lights were bright in there. Amos Bittner sat with his hands over his head.

Angelo grabbed my sleeve.

"Come on," he said. "Your car."

He went around the corner, not running, not walking, sort of gliding, soundless and quick. I did my best, but I was a little clumsy with my bad leg. He had the car door open when I got there and we slid into the back seat. He held the door to without latching it. He whispered to the driver. The driver started the motor, went into gear and got moving all at once. I don't know how he did it. We swung around in a wide U-turn and headed into Front Street. We came up behind the McCreery car, standing now in the street, opposite the bank.

It was forty feet from where Angelo crouched on the floor of the back seat to where Max stood with Singer on the steps of the bank. It was forty feet, an upward angle and with practically no room to maneuver. But I saw it with my own eyes. I saw Angelo push the car door open, set himself on his haunches, twist and shoot out his throwing arm. I saw Max stiffen, look straight up, drop his gun and keel over on his face.

Angelo tossed a lighted cigarette out of the car window in a wide arc toward the bank. Then he tapped the driver on the shoulder.

"Bump that car ahead hard," he said. "Then get the hell out of here back to where we were."

I braced myself. There was a heavy shock as the driver slammed into McCreery's car ahead, another when he backed, lurching, and still another when he went into low gear again and swung straight across the street to park beside the hardware store where we had been originally.

It had happened so fast I couldn't see everything that went on. Now, racing after Angelo, who had started back to the store front, I heard shooting.

We stood a moment, catching our breath, getting straightened out.

"You got a gun?" Angelo said.

"Yeah," I said.

"Can you shoot it?"

"Some."

"You got to cover that McCreery."

Two of Fortunata's men were making their way toward the bank entrance, close to the building fronts. Two more came around the corner out of the alley that ran beside the bank. They stopped there. McCreery would see them from the car at any moment.

I couldn't see McCreery, at first. Then his head lifted in the front seat. I let fly at him. The glass in the car window cracked and his head went down. I couldn't tell whether I'd hit him.

"Come on," Angelo said.

He ran into the street in a low crouch and I followed him. I saw the two Fortunata lads from the alley move up to the bank entrance. One of them leaned down, pulled the knife out of Max's chest and cut the rope between Singer's ankles. Then I couldn't look any more because we were at McCreery's car and Angelo was pulling the front door open.

McCreery charged out right into us, shooting as he came. But he was all mixed up. Angelo grabbed him by the coat collar and pulled him into the street. I kicked the gun out of his hand.

The back door of the car opened and the Burton woman climbed out. She streaked for the gun and got hold of it. Angelo kicked McCreery in the head and I went after Mrs. Burton. She was heading for the other Illinois car parked beside the limousine. She heard me behind her, shifted suddenly and went up on the walk. I tried to shift with her, but my bad leg gave out and I fell down.

There was more shooting at the bank entrance. I was scared for Singer, but I had to trust the Fortunata crew. Mrs. Burton had doubled back again and was climbing under the wheel of the car when I caught up with her. She stuck the gun right in my face and pulled the trigger. It didn't go off. I reached in and clipped her on the jaw. She slumped down in the seat against the wheel.

I went back to where Angelo stood over McCreery. Together we lifted him and carried him up onto the walk in front of the bank.

The two beefy boys came down the bank steps, their hands high in the air. The Fortunata crew were behind them. One of them carried a suitcase. He set it down near McCreery.

Singer Batts shuffled up to where we stood, the loose ends of the rope dragging behind his ankles. He looked down at McCreery.

"Are you all right, Joseph?" he asked quietly.

"Yeah. How are you?"

He gave me a long look. "I'm sick to death of violence," he said.

Caesar Fortunata walked with dignity along the sidewalk and joined us. Mr. Moynahan came up too. Singer looked at him and pointed to the suitcase.

"That is part of the money that was embezzled from the Spark-EE Corporation," he said.

Moynahan was mopping his face.

"They killed Nick Andrews," I said to Singer.

"McCreery?" he said.

"Yes."

Singer looked very tired. In a low, monotonous, almost wistful voice, he said, "Gentlemen, you will excuse me if I go to my room. For those of you who are interested, I will try to explain what has happened and why, a little later. Someone will please see to Amos Bittner."

He walked away across the street, shambling, the ropes dragging behind him. Nobody said anything. Even Fortunata just stood and watched him go.

CHAPTER XX

I went over to Fiske's Funeral Home and got Charlie Fiske to help us with the cleaning up. He took Max over to his preparation room. We borrowed a couple of stretchers. We put McCreery on one and Mrs. Burton on the other. Fortunata's men carried them over to the hotel. Angelo and two of his boys took McCreery's giants down to the jail. I went into the bank.

Amos was all right. He'd been slugged in the head and it took a while to bring him to. I asked him whether he wanted to come over to the hotel, but he said he guessed he'd go home. I helped him out to the car and he could drive all right.

There were still some people from town standing about and I told them to come around in the morning and I'd tell them what I could.

It took about an hour altogether and then everything was off the street and the cars were all parked where they should be and the town was quiet again, the way it is most of the time.

I went back to the hotel.

It was like a morgue in there. The two stretchers were sitting in the lobby and Fortunata's men were standing around. Fortunata himself stood a little apart from the others, Angelo close beside him. Moynahan had sat down in a deep leather chair. He was staring at the suitcase and sometimes at Mrs. Burton. Jack Pritchard sat at the desk, blinking. Somehow, the rat-faced man had disappeared. I guessed he'd been taken to the can along with the other two.

Singer wasn't in sight.

"Is there a bar in this town?" one of Fortunata's men asked.

"Downstairs," I said. "Beer and wine only. Hard liquor you have to get in the package."

"We'll have some beer," he said.

They all went out and I heard them going down to the tavern under the hotel.

Their absence gave the lobby a deserted appearance. Fortunata and Angelo; McCreery and Mrs. Burton on stretchers; Moynahan and Jack Pritchard were the only ones left.

"Your boys are efficient," I said to Fortunata.

"Naturally," he said. He sat down on one of the leather sofas and crossed his legs.

After looking McCreery over, I called Doc Blane, who had just got in from a call. He said he would be glad to come right down. I knew he wouldn't be glad at all, but he was an obliging guy. McCreery was losing blood at quite a pace and he was one I wanted to live through whatever he had coming to him. And whatever that was, I planned to be in on it.

Mrs. Burton wasn't so bad off as McCreery but she wasn't pretty any more. Her face had been badly damaged by McCreery and also by me when I had clipped her. She opened her eyes and saw me looking at her and I gave her a cigarette. She lay still on her back, smoking and staring at the ceiling.

McCreery groaned when Doc Blane began to examine him. Once he tried to roll away, out from under Doc's hands, and I pushed him back down, not too gently. Doc looked up at me.

"Take it easy, Joe," he said. "He's badly hurt."

"Not so badly," I said.

Doc went on with his work. I glanced at Mrs. Burton. She put out her cigarette and was watching.

"Will he die?" she asked me in a matter-of-fact voice.

"I hope not," I said.

"Listen—" she said softly and I said, "Shut up," and walked away.

"Where is Mr. Batts?" Fortunata asked.

"Mr. Batts is taking a well-earned rest," I said. "He will appear in due time."

"I don't like to wait," Fortunata said.

"I'm sorry. Mr. Moynahan can fill you in on some of the background."

Moynahan seemed glad to have a chance to talk. He explained about the embezzlement from his corporation, beginning with Antonio Perotta.

Fortunata interrupted. "I heard about that. I want to know how the Cipriano girls came to be killed."

"I'm not sure I know," Moynahan said. "The embezzlement began in 1941. Antonio Perotta must have killed Angora. Of course, he would have to put the money somewhere and I guess he gave it to his wife, Constancia. I am sure now that McCreery was his accomplice, was in on it with him."

"The phony confession we found," I said, "was written on McCreery's typewriter."

"Yes," Moynahan said.

"Who recommended McCreery to you as an honest shamus?" I asked.

"Someone at the insurance company. Mr. Prickett, I believe."

"Mr. Prickett is not a good judge of men."

The door of our private suite opened and Singer came into the lobby. He looked at Fortunata. "Thank you for saving my life," he said.

Fortunata waved his hand. "I have an engagement in a few hours in Chicago. If you don't mind, I would like to keep it."

"Certainly," Singer said. He looked wearily at the floor.

"Charles Angora died in 1940," Singer said at last. "From the day of his death until just the other day, the firm known as the Spark-EE Corporation paid him a monthly royalty of between seven and ten thousand dollars. For almost ten years, that is, the firm paid a royalty to a man who no longer existed. This was the beginning of the crime."

"All right, all right," Angelo broke in. "Who killed Marcella?"

"Don't be in a hurry," I said. "Before Marcella was killed, there was Constancia."

"Quite right," Singer said, "and they both died from the same cause. Murder for money.

"I know now," Singer said, "that Antonio Perotta did not initiate the embezzlement. Someone else had begun it. Antonio was an intelligent boy. He began to wonder about this huge royalty that was paid to Angora each month, in cash. He went to the Angora house, and he discovered that the royalties were going into another's pocket. He discovered that Angora was dead."

"This was McCreery?" Fortunata asked.

Singer ignored the question.

"Antonio decided to get some of the stolen money for himself. A pact was made. The price of Antonio's silence was a percentage of the money stolen so far and half of it thereafter. I believe that would account more or less correctly for the amount we found in the suitcase."

"Just a moment—" Moynahan interrupted.

His lips were working as if he had been doing some rapid calculating in his head.

"Yes?" Singer said.

"You say," Moynahan said, "that the embezzlement started in 1940 at the time of Angora's death. At the rate you are figuring on, the amount in the suitcase by this time would be almost twice as much as two hundred thousand dollars."

Singer looked at him. "You are correct, Mr. Moynahan," he said. "If the embezzlement had been carried on from 1940 to the present day on the same terms under which Antonio Perotta entered the scheme, the total amount by this time would exceed two hundred thousand dollars. Now, there is one point I would like to mention before I go on to explain about the money.

"Naturally, in order to make sure that the death of Angora would not come to light, the original embezzler undertook to keep up the Angora property so that it would not be obvious that nobody lived there any more. He hired Mrs. Burton for that job."

I glanced at Mrs. Burton. Her eyes were on Singer. She didn't bat an eye.

"Antonio," Singer went on, "to insure himself against any possible loss by cheating, took over the job of delivering the royalties to Angora's house.

"Then he was drafted. Theoretically, that removed him as a threat to the original thief. However, as long as Antonio lived, he would be a witness against the embezzler and this was obvious to the subject. An agreement was made, therefore, by which the original embezzler was to continue to pay the—'hush money,' I believe it's called—to Antonio's wife."

"The Cipriano sisters," Fortunata persisted. "Why were they killed?"

It was as if Singer hadn't heard his voice.

"To make doubly sure of his hold over the original thief," he said, "Antonio wrote a letter exposing the former's part in the plot. He gave the letter to his wife, Constancia, and the embezzler knew this."

Everybody was listening carefully. Moynahan was sitting on the edge of his seat. Mrs. Burton's fingers were stiff and poised. Only Fortunata sat in what seemed to be complete relaxation, while Angelo paced up and down the lobby silently, now and then glaring at Singer.

"Antonio was killed," Singer said. "And Antonio's wife, who knew the identity and character of the embezzler, went into panic. With no thought except to get away, she left Chicago and, as far as the thief was concerned, disappeared."

Angelo made a growling sound in his throat. He was impatient. So was I. McCreery had stirred a couple of times on the stretcher and I kept my eye on him closely.

"Since the embezzler did not know the whereabouts of Constancia," Singer said, "he could not make the payments. Antonio died in 1945. From that time until just a few days ago, the royalties continued to be delivered to Angora's house, only instead of being split between the embezzler and Constancia, they all went into the one pocket. And this would have been all right except for one thing: the embezzler knew that Constancia still had the letter that would expose him as the thief. He had to get that letter."

I was looking at McCreery, whose eyes had flickered open. Singer was looking at him too.

"The embezzler probably had made a few hit-or-miss attempts to locate Constancia during the four years following Antonio's death. But at last he decided that it would have to be done definitely, finally and completely. So he hired an expert to find her and to regain possession of the letter. He hired McCreery. And McCreery a couple of weeks ago went to Washington and found Constancia and tried to get the incriminating document back. I imagine he told her that she could keep what money she had if she would turn over the letter."

"That's right," a new voice said and we all looked at Mrs. Burton.

She was sitting up on the stretcher now, looking straight ahead.

"The rat tried to kill me," she said. "He would have got away with it."

"Yes?" Singer said.

"I went with him to Washington. He said there was a lot of money to be made. I'd been going out with him for a while… We couldn't get anything out of the girl and when we got back from Washington, we found she had come to Chicago to visit her sister. McCreery went after her again."

"Was it McCreery," Singer said, "who sent you to Marcella Cipriano's apartment when Constancia was murdered, to look for the incriminating letter?"

"Yes," she said.

"And after that, when Marcella was murdered?"

"Yes."

"And you didn't find the letter?"

"No."

There was a pause.

"You are lying," Singer said.

She stared at him with her mouth open.

"You were going around, as you say, not only with McCreery, but also with the murderer of the Cipriano sisters. You have been playing one of them against the other for some time."

"No—"

"It was the murderer of the Cipriano girls who was waiting for you at the airport this afternoon. It was the murderer who called you on the telephone while we were in your apartment."

"No—"

"Why do you try to protect him?" Singer asked. "Do you have some hope that by informing against McCreery, you can get the murderer free? Do you think you might still get away to Mexico City with the money?"

She didn't say any more.

Singer's voice dropped low. He was looking at Fortunata.

"McCreery did not kill the Cipriano girls," he said. "As a private detective, he was hired to locate Constancia and the missing letter."

There was some creaking and I glanced at the other stretcher. McCreery was coming to life. He had himself up on one elbow, looking at Singer, when I saw him and moved over beside him. Singer paid no attention.

"In the course of his work for the murderer," he said, "McCreery found out about some things that led him to think he could blackmail his employer. He found out most of them from Mrs. Burton."

McCreery spoke up suddenly.

"Get me that doctor again," he said.

"You're all right," I said. "Relax."

There was a hush. Mr. Moynahan was sitting very still. Mrs. Burton was rigid on the stretcher. Angelo stood on the balls of his feet. He had the knife in his hand. I wondered when he'd retrieved it. Or maybe he carried a supply of them.

After a long time, Mrs. Burton turned her head slowly, very slowly, and looked at Moynahan.

"I guess it's all over," she said quietly.

Moynahan stared at her. He must have stared for a full minute. Then he got up and made a break for the front door.

Angelo got there first. The knife lay against Moynahan's throat.

"You did it," Angelo said. "You killed Constancia and Marcella."

Moynahan kept quiet. He was afraid to move his throat.

Singer walked across the lobby and pushed Angelo away. He stood in front of Moynahan, protecting him.

"The man has a right to a trial," Singer said. "He'll get that trial."

Angelo began cursing in Italian and lifted the knife. Now it pointed at Singer's throat. A new voice spoke up. Caesar Fortunata had joined the group.

"No, Angelo," he said. "Mr. Batts is wrong for us, but he is right for him. If you kill Mr. Moynahan—who cares? But if you kill Mr. Batts, you will never forget it the rest of your life. Come along now. We'll go home."

His voice was low, even gentle, as if he had been talking to an erring son. And as in the case of Lieutenant Morgan the day before, I understood something about Fortunata and about Angelo that otherwise I would not have understood.

Fortunata touched his hat, turned and walked out of the hotel. Angelo was trembling. He stared at Moynahan, and then he followed Fortunata. As he passed me I touched his shoulder.

"Don't worry," I said. "He won't get away."

He shrugged off my hand and walked out. He was a good man in a pinch. It was too bad he'd picked that profession. The way he went at it, he would have only a short life.

Moynahan slumped against the wall, staring across the lobby at Mrs. Burton.

"How did you know?" he asked.

Singer's voice was thin and low.

"By the red hair we found in the bed at Marcella's apartment. By the fact that only you could have let Mrs. Burton know we would call on her the night McCreery waited there for me. By the fact that, although Charles Angora had been dead since 1940 at the latest, you claimed to have records indicating that the embezzlement did not begin until 1941. This was because you couldn't admit that you knew when Angora died and you tried to synchronize Angora's death with the beginning of Antonio Perotta's employment by your firm."

"Give me a break," Moynahan was muttering, "just a couple of hours—"

"I'm sorry," Singer said. "I won't break faith with Angelo. I promised him you would go to trial. And to trial, sir, you will go."

George Cooler came into the lobby.

"Where the hell have you been?" I asked.

"This is my night off," George said. "I was over to Montpelier to the show."

"Of all nights," I said.

"Singer—" George said.

"Explanations later, George," Singer said. "You may lock up this gentleman, whose name is Moynahan."

George put handcuffs on Moynahan and led him away.

Everybody had been watching Angelo and Moynahan, including me, and suddenly, as the tension eased, a hunch made me turn. Then I was running across the lobby toward the rear corridor and the back door. I had not seen McCreery crawl off the stretcher, but I knew he had because now I was watching his back lurch away from me down that corridor.

He got through the service entrance into the alley and slammed the door on me hard enough to latch it, so I lost a couple of seconds.

Outside, he was smart enough not to turn left into the blind end of the alley. He ran toward the street. He ran halfway there and then he stopped suddenly. Somebody was blocking the way, standing there where the alley ran into the street, standing very still, with her arms straight down, her hands empty.

"Pat!" she said. "It's no use to run."

McCreery cursed. I was close behind him and he heard me. He jerked his head around once and then he lit out diagonally across the parking lot toward the street farther north.

He was running hard, but he was too far gone. My leg gave me some trouble, but I was better off than he was. Halfway across the lot he stumbled and when he got his balance he swayed back and forth and lost time.

I caught up with him just short of the sidewalk. His breath was loud now and every time he took a step, his knees gave way. I reached and got hold of his coat collar.

He had just enough fight left to swing once at me, very wide, very loose. I stepped in under the swing. I hit him three times in the stomach and he fell on my feet. I used one of them to roll him over. He didn't notice it.

Mrs. Burton came up the walk. She stopped and looked down at McCreery and then she looked at me.

"You got any idea of running?" I asked.

"No," she said.

"All right then," I said.

I put my fingers in my mouth and whistled three times. Mrs. Burton and I stood there in silence and McCreery lay still on the ground and after a long while, George Cooler came and took them both away.

I went back into the hotel.

* * * *

In the suite it was quiet. Singer sat in his Boston rocker, rocking gently back and forth.

"Carnage is over," I said.

"Yes, Joseph," he said.

I mixed myself a stiff drink. I heard a very unusual sound—a chuckling sound. I glanced over toward Singer. He was leaning back in the Boston rocker and he was chuckling, right out loud.

"What's funny?" I asked.

"I just happened to think about poor Amos Bittner," he said. "When those ruffians called him on the phone and told him they were holding me hostage until he opened the bank—"

"Yes?" I said. "This is killing me. Go on."

"They made me say something over the phone to him. I had to admit to Amos that everything they said was true. Amos was worried about opening the bank. And he said—you wouldn't guess what he said—"

"Please," I said.

"Amos said, 'I don't know what the Federal Reserve Board would say about it.'"

"That's very funny," I said, trying to laugh.

"I reminded him," Singer said, "that the Federal Reserve Board was a statistical unit, whereas at the moment we were dealing with people."

"It doesn't seem like much of a joke," I said.

"It is quite a joke, Joseph," he said. "It is a rare and wonderful joke that my life hung on the decision of a man who was worried about the attitude of the Federal Reserve Board."

"Ha, ha," I said. "I'll laugh in the morning. Good night."

"Good night, Joseph."

He was still chuckling as I walked into the bedroom and began to get undressed.